THE FOOTSTEPS ON THE STAIRS

BY THE SAME AUTHOR:

GO, LOVELY ROSE

DEATH OF A STRAY CAT

THE DIEHARD

THE MAN WITH THE CANE

BLOOD WILL TELL

HOME IS THE PRISONER

THE EVIL WISH

THE ONLY GOOD SECRETARY

THE FOOTSTEPS ON THE STAIRS

by

JEAN POTTS

LONDON
VICTOR GOLLANCZ LTD
1967

Printed in Great Britain by
Lowe & Brydone (Printers) Ltd., London

THE FOOTSTEPS ON THE STAIRS

chapter 1

Four years after they had said Goodbye Forever in Philadelphia—life being what it is, a mesh of dangling threads—they met again, at a press party in New York. One of the Glasbrix publicity staff, an overwrought girl in a flower-bucket hat, introduced them. Enid Baxter. "She does the most divine interiors, Vic sweetie, simply fabulous." And Victor Holm. "Mark my word, Enid dear, some day we're all going to say we knew him when. He designs the most fabulous houses. Simply divine."

"How do you do," said Vic.

Enid waited until the flower-bucket hat had been washed back into the main stream. "I'm ahead of the crowd. I already knew you when." Her first impulse, to turn and run, passed; she felt remarkably calm, especially after noting the wobble in Vic's hand as he held a light for her cigarette.

"It's been a long time," he said. "Not that you look a day older."

He did. His sandy hair, though it was still thick, was frosted with white. All the way through, no longer just at the temples. His ruddy, blunt-featured face was not the type to wrinkle, but she saw—it hurt her to see—the first subtle blurring, the token of sagging to come. And there was something different about his eyes. They were the same hazy gray, of course; dreamer's eyes, she used to think. Different dreams now, maybe. Or it could well be that the change was in her own eyes more than in Vic's. This amazing calm of hers. She was proud of it. But a little saddened, too: she had been so sure that Vic was the one she would never get over.

"You're looking very well," she said kindly. At least he hadn't gotten fat. He had the stocky, sturdy build of a peasant; it made him seem shorter than he actually was. Enid tilted her head to smile at him. "I'm glad to hear you're going places."

"That's me. Always en route. Never quite getting there."

"Maybe you aim too high."

"Not any more," he said grimly. "I'm strictly a money-grubber these days. It may not be soul-satisfying, but it's a damn sight more comfortable."

"If you say so. I just dabble myself." She was quoting him; her freedom from financial worries had always enraged him. Even now, she thought, observing the spark of temper in his face. "I don't have the professional attitude."

"I know, I've kept track of you. Especially now that I'm in New York too."

"You are?" She felt the first ominous tremor. His use of the first person singular signified nothing, of course; he was an expert at ignoring Thelma's existence. When it suited his convenience. And anyway, Enid assured herself, his present marital status was a matter of supreme indifference to her. She didn't care where he lived, either; certainly New York was big enough for both of them. "When did that happen?"

"Three or four months ago. Matter of fact, we're practically neighbors."

"Really? It's a small world, as they say."

"Very small. But then you knew as well as I did that wasn't the end, that day in Philadelphia. We were bound to run across each other again sooner or later. Just a question of time."

"I never had any such notion," she lied. "As I recall that day in Philadelphia, you sounded pretty final."

"*I* sounded final! You were the one. Didn't I beg you not to get on that train to New York? But no. You walked away and left me—I can still see you, switching off in that damn purple suit—and you never looked back, not even so much as a glance."

Naturally not; it would have been fatal. And how typical it was of Vic to insist, now as then, that the breakup was entirely her doing, no responsibility whatever of his. When the truth was that the crucial decision had been his alone. For the choice he had made—Thelma instead of her; that was what it amounted to, whether he admitted it or not—left her with no alternative except to get on the train to New York. Walk away and leave him, as he put it, and never look back.

Only here they were again, face to face. Yes, and he was looking pleased with himself, as if he knew all about the tremor she had imagined she was hiding so successfully. "How's Thelma?" she asked, to even the score.

His face stiffened, and at that moment Thelma's famous laugh rang out. Her trademark: that delightful, delighted laugh, uninhibited as a child's, and because it was the thing about Thelma that had rankled most, Enid was now acutely aware of the change in it. It no longer rang true. The bell was cracked.

"There she is," said Vic. "Over by the window."

Apparently her taste in clothes had improved. (Well. Nowhere to go but up.) She was wearing quite a smart dress, deep blue, good with her eyes, and cleverly cut, good with her tall, willowy figure. Even the hat wasn't too bad, except for the veil. Enid remembered her hair, which she still wore in bangs, as being a duller shade of brown. Had she taken to touching it up? It seemed out of character. So did the clothes, when it came to that. The Thelma of four years ago had been blithely unconcerned about such matters.

She was talking—not to the customary cluster of people who used to gather around her like tacks drawn to a magnet—but to one lone young man, who in spite of his polite smile was clearly on the lookout for an escape route. His eyes darted this way and that, he made nervous, unsuccessful little attempts to edge away from Thelma's hand on his sleeve. A tableau of desperation: his growing restiveness spurred her on to more and more anxious animation. The charming Mrs. Victor Holm, thought Enid, not quite so charming nowadays.

But the spark of wry triumph she might have felt flickered out at once. Vic too was watching his wife, inspecting her with coldly clinical interest, as if she were a specimen under a microscope. "Don't look like that," Enid said sharply.

"Like what? I'm just gauging the saturation level. One more drink and I'll have to get her home."

Thelma a lush? But she used to drink hardly at all. Hadn't needed to, any more than she had needed to bother much about the right clothes or make-up. So why should she turn to drink now? After all, she was the winner. He had chosen her, not Enid.

The restive young man had escaped, in spite of all her efforts. She was left standing by herself, smiling (yes, a little glassily) at everyone and no one.

"Don't let me keep you," said Enid.

"Wait. Let's get out of here. Go some place where we can talk—"

"What about? It's all been said. It's all over. I have a dinner date, anyway. Not to mention your other obligations."

"Trust you to mention them, though. You haven't changed, have you?"

"The point is that I have," she said. "You don't know me any more. Wouldn't like me if you did."

"Who's talking about liking? That's a nothing of a word to use about us."

All right. Yes. They had either loved each other or hated each other. The heights or the depths. No golden mean. "Makes no difference now," she said, and smiled brilliantly into the distance.

"We'll see about that. Later, then. After this dinner date of yours. I'll ring your bell."

"Thank you for warning me. I won't answer it."

"I'll take a chance," he said. "I walk past your house often, and there's your name under the mailbox, and the bell— Once I actually rang it, but there wasn't any answer."

"Naturally not. I never answer anonymous doorbell rings."

"Very sensible of you. A woman living alone can't be too careful. Assuming, of course, that you are living alone. . ." He paused, his eyes hardening. He had always been jealous, even in the days when he had no reason to be. On top of that, had dismissed her resentment of Thelma as utter nonsense. He had no claim on her now. Let him stew. "That's quite a place, the house you're living in," he went on. "Straight out of Chas Addams. Is it as spooky inside as out?"

"Spookier. I love it." Vic would be enchanted with it: she could see him in the middle of her living room, peering at the chandelier that hung like a stalactite from the cavernous ceiling, at the dim, full-length mirror with its ornate gold frame, at the marble fireplace and wide floor boards that creaked underfoot and gleamed like brown satin. She could hear his delighted chuckle when he spotted the hand-painted door knobs. Hastily she pulled the damper on her imagination. He was never going to see any of it, and that was that.

"Do you still have that misbegotten love seat, and the cabbage patch rug?"

She nodded. And the afghan they used to lie under on chilly evenings; the bronze clock that had chimed off the precious fleeting hours. The brandy snifters were long since broken, though, and the lone survivor of their favorite coffee cups was handleless, gathering dust on the top shelf, because she could not bring herself to throw it out. Until now: she would go home tonight and get rid of it. Her years of bondage were over, this final encounter with Vic was a necessary part of the ritual of release. With it behind her, the cycle was complete, she was once more her own woman. And about time, too. When she thought of those first black months when she had carried wherever she went the leaden burden of her heart; of the terrible, rare evenings alone when she had stared at the telephone, battling the urge to pick it up, obsessed with listening—for it to ring, even more tensely (and illogically) for the sound of his footstep on the stairs. . .

"Enid," he said. "My little blackbird." His hand touched hers, and she pulled away in terror of the remembered current. It was still there, still there; she had not been quick enough. "Just for a little while. An hour. Half an hour. Please, Enid, please."

"Don't. No, no." She got her voice back under control. "Nice to see you, Vic. Good luck." She moved off, waggling her fingers at him, smiling a cocktail-party smile, and resolutely avoiding his eyes.

The cracked bell of Thelma's laugh rang out again, summoning him.

Even so, Enid left before they did. (She had not been lying about the dinner date. It was only with Martin, but it would serve.) As she was going out the door, she caught sight of them, halfway across the room; Vic had a firm grip on Thelma's elbow and seemed to be reasoning with her, in a patient, practiced way. He did not see Enid. But Thelma did. Her veil was askew; through its cross-hatchings, as through the barbed wire of a concentration camp, she stared out—empty-eyed at first, then, after the click of recognition, sick with fear. She caught her slack lower lip between her teeth, and her hand moved vaguely, in a gesture that was half-defensive, half-pleading.

Enid turned and hurried out. She was trembling with resentment—against herself for pitying Thelma, against Thelma for provoking the pity. What right had she to work on Enid's sympathies? She was the winner, Enid insisted to herself; Vic was hers, all hers, always had been, always would be. Thelma had no excuse for going into such a panic. As if Enid were some kind of a monster or, even worse, a fool who didn't know when she was licked. Well, she did know. And furthermore knew when she was well off: free at last from the spell Vic had cast over her. She was a different person now (imagine feeling sorry for Thelma four years ago!) and so was he (oh yes, it showed in his eyes) and it was no use trying to get back to what they used to be and feel. That old cure-all time had done its work, no matter how determined Vic might be to pretend otherwise. She was realistic enough to face the truth, if he wasn't. The bitterly sad truth; during the cab ride downtown she gave way to a fit of weeping. But this way at least her image of Vic-and-Enid as they had once been would remain intact, unspoiled by the overlay of what they were now. For she knew it would be spoiled. Their heyday was in the past; to try to recapture it now would lead to anticlimax at best, quite possibly to something much more disastrous. She knew it, she knew it.

How did it happen, then, that three hours later she sat on the misbegotten love seat—alone; both she and Martin had been in favor of an early evening—once more obsessed with waiting? Only tonight she waited for a certainty: the doorbell was bound to ring. Vic hadn't changed that much. The question was whether she had changed enough to let it go unanswered. But if so, why was she here at all when she could so easily have dodged the whole issue? That might be precisely the point—to put herself to the test and settle the matter, once and for all. An attractive theory. She grew more and more attached to it.

When the doorbell rang she rose like a sleepwalker and pushed the buzzer. It was beside the door, as the buzzer in her Philadelphia apartment had been, and she stayed there, as she used to do in the old days, listening for the sound of his step on the stairs. She would have known it anywhere: the same quick, heavy thud, with her heart pounding in time. Like Pavlov's dogs. Her hand rose of its own accord and released the bolt, opened the door. They were in each other's arms—more of a collision than an embrace—and for one tremulous moment she could almost believe that nothing was changed and they were back in their lost heyday.

Then she pulled free enough to look up into his eyes.

chapter 2

One evening a week later Martin Shipley rang Enid's bell—three rings: their signal—to explain that he had locked himself out of his ground-floor apartment and needed the key he had planted with her against this recurrent emergency.

"Come on up." Her answer over the house phone was prompt and cheerful if a little breathless, he thought as he bounded up the stairs. Maybe she had just gotten home herself.

He was disconcerted and embarrassed to discover, when she opened her door, that she had a guest. She knew how he was about meeting strangers, but instead of simply handing him the key, she insisted on ushering him inside and introducing him to the man who was standing beside the fireplace. A big man, as tall as Martin and much broader, with a ruddy, open face and a shock of sandy-gray hair.

So this was Victor Holm. To Martin the name was

more than familiar; in Enid's confidential reminiscences it figured as the major theme on which she played her endless variations of tenderness, grief, anger and longing. (As the name of Joyce figured in Martin's memories.) But somehow he had never attached the name of Victor Holm to a body, a real flesh-and-blood man whom he might some day meet face to face. It was as if a legendary character had suddenly materialized.

"Martin's my neighbor," Enid was explaining gaily. "He has the first-floor apartment. Horticulture brought us together."

It was true enough. Enid had her terrace; Martin the scrap of soil outside his front windows where ivy and a few spindly bushes—left-overs from the previous tenant—struggled to survive. Their friendship had begun with an exchange of nods when, on her way in or out of the house, Enid would see him grubbing there; had progressed to small pleasantries that bloomed, along with Martin's morning glories, into their first real conversation. It was a curiously fast friendship, considering their surface disparities. For Enid kept her loneliness hidden, while Martin's was there for all the world to see; he wore it like a mourning band.

"Horticulture?" Victor Holm bared his teeth in a hostile smile. "How nice."

A jealous type, just as Enid had reported. Poor devil, thought Martin complacently. He had no more designs on Enid than she had on him. Still, the idea of himself as a romantic rival was decidedly pleasant. Feeling very much at ease, quite a man of the world, in fact, he accepted the drink Enid pressed on him, settled down in the easy chair, and lit a cigarette.

She was shamelessly enjoying the situation. He had

never seen this side of her, and it intrigued him to watch her playing the female primeval instead of the understanding older sister he was used to. What a charmer she was! Like an ivory and jet figurine come to life—her face sparkling with the vivacity it sometimes lacked, her every gesture full of provocative grace. She was wearing a wide-sleeved robe splashed with colors brilliant as a bird's plumage.

"Martin's with a publishing company, Vic," she said. "He edits textbooks. He just finished one on architecture."

"Bully for him," said Vic, and rattled his ice cubes.

"I'm so sorry you can't stay for another drink, darling. You and Martin would have so much to talk about. Maybe another time. When you and Thelma aren't going to the theater. Do remember me to her, won't you? And have fun."

"You too," said Vic. "Lots of nice neighborly fun." He bared his teeth again on the way out.

When Enid came back from seeing him to the door, Martin said, "What a little bitch you are."

"Only because he asks for it. Can you imagine? He was jealous of you! Not that you're not attractive, of course," she added, and patted his hand. "If you were ten years older he might have a point."

"Thanks." He had no illusions about his own weedy, knobby appearance. Even Joyce had never considered him handsome. If she had loved him at all, it was in spite of his looks. "You're pretty irresistible yourself. For an old lady. How long has Victor the Great been back in your life?"

"He's not. I mean, not really." She shot him a queer, defiant look. "Well. What did you think of him?"

"He surprised me. Though I don't know exactly what I expected. Somebody smoother, I guess. Not such a wholesome farmer type."

"That's what I thought too, when I first met him. If only people's insides matched their outsides! Vic looks so solid, so steady and forthright, when the truth is he's the most confused, the most unstable—" She dropped down on the love seat, weary now, her face drained of the animation that had transfigured it. Martin recognized that withdrawn, mask-like look; he had seen her through more than one fit of what she called The Despondencies. "Even more so than four years ago. It's worse. Much worse. I wish I'd never seen him again!"

"You don't have to go on seeing him," Martin offered, without conviction. "If he upsets you so much, why not just drop him?"

"Because I never do the right thing, that's why not. Or if I do, it's at the wrong moment. It sounds so easy. Just drop him. Don't see him any more. You don't know Vic. You don't know how he is."

"Of course, if you're still in love with him—"

"Not the way I was. It's all spoiled now. All changed." She stared down at her hands. She was wearing, as always, the ring Vic had given her, a gold band set with squares of jade. A little too heavy for a hand as delicate as Enid's, in Martin's opinion. She had a nervous habit of twisting it round and round. "I feel sorry for him, Martin, and I can't bear it. I can't bear to feel sorry for Vic!"

"Sorry for him? Hell, you were needling him for all you were worth."

"Of course I was. I have to needle him. Because— Oh, what's the use? You'd never understand people like Vic and me. You're too sane."

"Who, me?" It was not the first time she had cast aspersions on his insanity. He suspected her of therapeutic motives, and was all the more nettled. "I'm sicker in the head than you or Vic ever dreamed of being. Just ask Joyce's parents."

"Okay, okay. They think you're crazy. But they didn't convince anybody else."

"Only me," said Martin. "A trifling detail. Hardly worth mentioning."

"Exactly. Because it's not true. If you really thought you were a maniac you'd keep your dark and dreadful past to yourself instead of pouring it out to me. It's not so dark and dreadful, anyway. You've talked yourself into all this guilt business about Joyce just because—"

"Please. Spare me the pep talk. I've heard it before."

"I was going to give you the revised version this time. But all right, I can take a hint." She laughed light-heartedly. When he first knew her these rapid swings in mood had bewildered him; now he was used to them. "Let's have another drink. Would you like to stay for dinner? There's some chicken I'd love to get rid of. I promise not to try to cheer you up."

"Fine. Great." This time the therapeutic motives were his: the more casual Enid was with her invitations the more sincerely she meant them. She disliked admitting that she did not want to be alone. Besides, he had nothing else to do. As usual. His friends had all been his and Joyce's; he had no heart for finding new ones.

Neither of them mentioned Victor Holm until dinner was over and they were having coffee and brandy on the terrace. It was a balmy, starry April evening. The people in the next-door garden were cooking hamburgers, and the smoke wafted up, mingling with the smell of Enid's geraniums. The house backed on an office building, so on week ends and evenings the terrace was pleasantly quiet and secluded.

"The trouble is he's moved here," Enid said abruptly.

Martin did not ask who. He sipped his brandy and waited.

"They've moved here, I should say. He and Thelma. I gather she's turned into pretty much of a lush."

"So that's why you feel sorry for him."

"No, that's not why. After all, turn about's fair play. Oh yes, that was the thing, you see, he was a problem drinker himself at one time—years ago, before I knew him—and Thelma pulled him through like the loyal, long-suffering, true-blue helpmeet she is. So naturally he couldn't repay all that devotion by deserting her for me. Not to mention the fact that I was his on any terms, and let him know it. Like the fool I was. Why didn't I see it in time? I could have done it, I could have saved him."

"Saved him from what? What are you talking about?"

"He could have been a good architect, Martin, I mean really good. He had originality and flair and this tremendous enthusiasm. He's lost it now, somehow it's all gone, and he doesn't even *care!*" She beat her fists on her knees. "All he wants is money. Security. He's not willing to try anything new any more, for fear of being called a screwball—that's what he was, in a way, but a brilliant one—and he was almost over the hump, a few more years of developing his own ideas and he would have made it. He's let it all go, settled for this job that's never going to lead anywhere, why, he won't even keep it, once they realize he hasn't got the zing they hired him for!"

"And you think you could have kept him on the upward path. Is that it?"

"I know how it sounds. But all the same. . . We

sparked each other. Call it love, sex, chemistry, whatever. It was there, and it was great. I never *admired* any man the way I did Vic. With all the others, I called the shots. Because I was brainier or stronger or maybe just meaner. But with Vic. . ."

"Well, all you have to do is say the word. Here he is again, obviously bent on picking up where you and he left off—"

"Wrong again. What he's bent on now is marrying me." She laughed bitterly. "How's that for irony? Four years too late he's all mine. Four years too late. I was dying to marry him then. That's why I came to New York, because I couldn't stand not having him all to myself. And now when I don't want him any more he's all at once determined to ditch Thelma for me."

"I'm not so sure you don't want him any more," said Martin cautiously. "There must be something left or you wouldn't be in such a state."

"Of course there's something left. Bed. And I'm not belittling it. I don't object to having an affair with Vic, picking up where we left off, as you put it. But I won't marry him. I couldn't possibly. I told you, I don't admire him now, I don't even respect him, I feel *sorry* for him! Because he missed the boat and either doesn't know it or won't admit it. He thinks he can go back and do it right this time, but he can't, nobody ever can. Thinks I can wave some kind of a magic wand and give him back what he threw away, but I can't, I can't. . . Let's have another brandy."

In the darkness her face was only a blur, magnolia-white, with smudges for her eyes, which he knew must be filled with tears, and her mouth, which he knew must be trembling. He could think of nothing to say: she was too proud for comfort, too headstrong for advice. And as always he was too slow-witted; the right words would come to him hours from now, when they could do no good. That was the story of his life.

When she spoke again, it was in a different voice, calm and reflective. "You know, Martin, there's something else. It occurred to me the other night that Vic might be dangerous."

"Dangerous! You mean he threatened you?"

"Of course. But then he's threatened me before. Too often to remember. The battles we used to have! I gave him a beauty of a black eye once. My finest hour."

"Oh well." Martin sank back in relief. "Battles. I thought you meant—"

"I did. I do. I think it's possible Vic might some day kill me."

"What is this, anyway?" His heart beat thickly now, with belated anger. And a sense of betrayal; she had led him on, lured him into trusting her, while all the time she was secretly harboring the same suspicions everyone else had about him. "Your idea of a joke? Or some kind of a trick? You already know all I know about Joyce. What the hell are you trying to do?"

"Oh, stop it. Don't be so touchy. Who's talking about Joyce? You always twist everything around to her. You won't let yourself or anybody else forget it."

"You think it's that easy? Forget it. Shrug it off. It didn't happen to you."

"I know, Martin." She stretched out her hand, and after an instant's hesitation he took it. Such a small hand, but strong and warm, full of life. "Honestly, honestly. No tricks. And no jokes. Anything but."

"Listen, Enid, if you really think this guy is going to kill you—"

"Now, now. I just mentioned the possibility. Very remote. And anyway, it would be my own fault, for needling him into it."

"But my God, you mustn't see him again! I don't care if it's just a possibility. You thought of it. It crossed your mind. That's enough for me. Too much. You simply must not see him again."

She withdrew her hand. "I'm sure you're right," she said politely.

"Promise me. Promise me."

"But I might not keep my word. You wouldn't want to make a liar of me, would you?" She gave a teasing, affectionate laugh. "What's so terrible about dying? It happens to everybody some time, somehow. I'm not all that enchanted with life nowadays, anyway. No, and neither are you, if some of the things you've told me are true."

They were true, all right. "It's quite a different matter," he said stiffly, "going out of your way to get yourself murdered. In the first place—"

"Yes? Yes? I'm all ears."

"I can't believe you're serious! You must be kidding!"

"How can I resist it, with somebody as solemn as you? I declare, Martin, you should have been born an owl. You'd be so lovely stuffed. And then the brandy. I always develop these morbid fancies when I drink brandy. Shall we have another?"

"So you can get morbider and morbider? No, thanks."

"Okay." She yawned. "If you'll go home I'll go to bed."

"And dream about being stabbed, I suppose."

"No, I think strangled. Sweet dreams to you, too. I'll take the tray in, if you'll do the chairs."

"Yes, Ma'am." She was very orderly; the chairs had to be folded and stacked just so, in their special place against the wall. Martin had helped her build the little stile arrangement that led into the living room through the big window. Which he was careful to lock behind him. "Will that be all, Ma'am?"

"Your key. Remember? That's what you came for."

"So it is, so it is." He sometimes played up his absent-mindedness, which by turns irritated and amused her. It was nice, having her fuss over him. A wave of anxious tenderness for her surged through him; he turned at the door. "You really were just kidding me? You're sure now?"

She burst out laughing. "Owl. Always looking for something to brood about, aren't you? Just remember, don't you ever breathe a word of this to anybody, ever, under any circumstances. You do, and so help me, I'll come back and haunt you. That's if I'm dead. If I'm alive— Well, you'll wish I weren't."

"I'll never wish that. That's the whole point. I don't want—"

She was going on as if he had not spoken. "But then I know I can count on you. It's the wonderful thing about you, you never betray a confidence. I can say whatever pops into my head, no matter how wacky it is, and it's safe with you, you'll keep it to yourself. I mean, you always have. You're not going to start letting me down now, are you?"

"Of course I'm not going to let you down."

"Cross your heart? Hope to die?"

He looked down into her face: the round, willful forehead, the jet-brilliant eyes urgently holding his. "You win," he said after a moment. "Cross my heart."

He had promised, she hadn't, he thought as he went slowly down the stairs. He saw now the bargain he should have struck—her word not to see Vic again in exchange for his not to betray tonight's confidences. One more belated brain storm. He was running true to form.

chapter 3

"Morning, Mrs. Nicholson. Hot enough for you?" the doorman said as she hurtled—in a rush, as usual—out of her apartment building.

The cab driver explained, all the way across town, that it wasn't the heat, it was the humidity.

The elevator operator had a variation on the theme: "That thunderstorm last night didn't do a bit of good, did it? Made it worse, if anything."

It was that kind of a midsummer morning.

She opened the office door with its modest gold lettering: "Hazel Nicholson—Interiors" and drew in a grateful breath of air conditioning. Her daughter Rosemary, who was helping out during the summer, glanced up from the *Times* crossword puzzle long enough to say, "Hi, Mom. Tuck your blouse in. You look broiled."

Hazel knew it; she had caught a glimpse of herself in the plate glass window downstairs as she got out of the cab. Red, moist face under wilting gray hair; figure blocky and waistless as a mailbox, solidly based on the clumps of her space shoes. Rosemary herself, of course, looked as fresh and crisp and slim as a stalk of celery.

"Coffee?" she asked. "I got two containers."

"No time." Hazel mopped her neck and dropped her bag, bulging with upholstery samples, on the desk. "The newly weds will be here any minute, breathing down my—"

"They're not coming," said Rosemary. "They decided to stay out at the beach another day. Too hot to drive into town. They hoped you'd understand." She added virtuously, "I tried to call you at home, but you must have just left."

All that mad rush for nothing. Well, Hazel was used to it. She settled down with the other container of coffee, opened the dog-eared notebook in which she kept track of jobs pending, and prepared to revise her day's schedule. Five minutes of companionable silence, except for Rosemary: "Hero of silent films. Long. Begins with B," and Hazel: "Barthelmess. Don't they teach you anything in college?"

Then the phone rang. "Hazel Nicholson Interiors," Rosemary warbled into it. "One moment, please." She put her hand over the mouthpiece and whispered, "Some guy for you. Sergeant somebody? I didn't catch his name."

Neither did Hazel. His name didn't matter. His message did. She listened, aware of the sweat chilling on her brow, and of Rosemary's eyes fixed on her, round with apprehension.

"Something's happened to Enid," she said when she had hung up. "An accident, he said. A bad accident. They want me to come down there to her apartment."

"I'm coming with you."

"Don't be silly." She stood up heavily and found, to her surprise and embarrassment, that her legs were so wobbly she had to steady herself against the desk. "No need for us both to go. He sounded so— Rosemary, I think it's very bad."

"Let's go," said Rosemary. "What exactly did he *say*, Mom?" she demanded when they were on their way downtown in the cab. "Tell me everything he said."

"Well, he said he understood I was Enid Baxter's—partner? No, business associate, I think that was the way he put it. And of course I am, so I said yes, and a good friend of hers too, from way back. So then he said, 'I'm sorry to inform you that Miss Baxter has met with an accident. We would appreciate it if you would come down to her apartment at once.' It must be the police. The way he said 'we.' And it can't be a car accident or she wouldn't be at home. I know that's where most accidents happen, in the home, but then why in the world haven't they gotten her to a hospital? Why waste time calling me if. . . You heard me asking what's happened, what kind of an accident, how serious? That's when he said a bad accident, and I would be informed of the details when I got there. And that's all. That's every solitary word I got out of him."

Rosemary's hand tightened on hers, giving comfort, but no doubt seeking it too. When she was in her early teens Rosemary had set Enid apart on a little pedestal of her own. Labeled Sophistication, Hazel supposed, or Glamour; qualities conspicuously lacking in her mother. The gifts Enid gave her were treasured. (And few and far between. She did not know about the pedestal. Children and adolescents bored her.) Enid's most casual comments were seized upon as pearls of wisdom; her mannerisms clumsily, touchingly imitated. That stage was over now, thank God. Rosemary the adolescent had turned into still another stranger: a poised young woman with a brand-new college degree and a mind of her own. But though Enid no longer occupied a pedestal, she still had her special niche, her special charm for Rosemary.

For Hazel too, when it came to that. With her the feeling was partly proprietary pride because she had given Enid her first job, and partly gratitude because four years ago Enid had turned to her again—on quite a different basis this time, with an established reputation, and with a modest legacy from her father's estate which she had eventually invested in Hazel's business. The arrangement was highly satisfactory for both of them: Hazel could afford to expand; Enid could work as a free lance on the jobs that interested her and skip those that didn't. "Business associates." The policeman, or whoever he was, had hit the nail on the head. In spite of the closeness of that association and the fifteen-year span of their friendship, Hazel knew very little about Enid's personal affairs. There had been an impulsive and ill-advised college marriage, already expiring when Enid first came to work for her. There had been a procession of "beaus," shadowy background characters more or less indistinguishable to Hazel. There had been, or so she gathered, an unfortunate love affair in Philadelphia. Enid had never chosen to confide. Hazel had never pried. And just as well, too; she somehow sensed that they would not see eye to eye on such matters.

In an odd way, she thought, Enid was a lonely sort of person. It was the first time such an idea had occurred to her. She decided not to mention it; Rosemary would give her one of those withering looks and say she was out of her mind.

There wasn't time, anyway. "We'd better get out here," she said when they reached the corner of Enid's block and saw all the police cars. The sight of them unnerved her; she had been prepared for only one. Cops swarmed in front of the old four-story brick house, ordering each other around, shooing curious passers-by on their way, now and then admitting somebody with the proper credentials. They let Hazel and Rosemary in eventually. Not, however, before the one word had leapt out at Hazel from a jumble of anonymous voices behind her. The one black word, murder.

She paused at the door and said weakly, "You wait down here for me, Rosemary. Honestly, I'd rather—"

"Don't be silly," said Rosemary. "Tuck your blouse in and come on."

There was a slight commotion as they and their police escort started up the stairs. It was caused by the arrival of the young man who lived on the first floor. (Hazel could not remember his name, though she had met him once at Enid's.) He had a suitcase in each hand. His expression was harried, and his voice was husky with fatigue and strain. "Certainly I live here. You saw my name on the mailbox. This is my apartment, right here. I'm just back from vacation, and I— What's happened? What's going on?"

The reply was mumbled; all Hazel caught of it was Enid's name. When she looked back from the landing she saw the young man propped against the wall—like something broken and discarded, an inside-out umbrella, she thought—his face white under the vacation tan, his eyes blank.

Murder. A black word down there on the street. In Enid's apartment a black reality. They had not taken her away yet; covered by a sheet, she lay beside the terrace window where her maid Carrie had found her when she came to work. The window stood open. Out on the terrace a handful of men milled about among the flower boxes and porch furniture. There were twinkling pools from last night's thunderstorm in the canvas seats of the chairs.

She had been stabbed, according to the gentle-voiced man who took charge of them, stabbed with a knife she used for cutting back bushes. They had found it on the terrace. If Mrs. Nicholson would be kind enough to identify. . . Hazel nodded dumbly. Nodded again when the sheet was pulled back briefly and she looked down at the small, sprawled body in the gay-flowered cotton dress and sandals. Enid's face had the drained, fragile look of a shell. Her eyes were not quite closed, slitted; her mouth, bright with lipstick, curved a little, so that she seemed to be smiling scornfully at death. Or perhaps at life.

Then the gentle-voiced man steered them into the bedroom, where he sat at the rosewood desk and they perched side by side on the chaise longue. Rosemary was crying fiercely, against her will. With Hazel it was her legs. Wobbling again, even after she sat down. But her voice was all right, steadily, matter-of-factly telling what she knew about Enid Baxter. She knew all the things that didn't matter—what Enid had paid for the chaise longue, for instance, where she had found the rug and the alabaster lamp, who had upholstered the boudoir chair. And none of the things that mattered. Acquaintances? Friends? Enemies? Only a few of the names in Enid's address book were familiar to her. She did not know about any love affair Enid was involved in. Could think of no one who might possibly have a motive for wanting her dead.

"We weren't that kind of friends," she said helplessly. "I mean not intimate in that way. It wasn't all business, of course. We often had lunch together, or a drink after work. Occasionally dinner. We were very fond of each other, but. . . It doesn't have to be someone she knew, does it? It could have been a burglar."

That was certainly a possibility, the detective agreed. In fact, there were a number of indications that Miss Baxter might have surprised a would-be thief in the act of sneaking in through the terrace window, whereupon the intruder panicked, killed her, and fled without stealing anything. Burglars, particularly amateurs, sometimes did just that.

Apparently Miss Baxter had gone down to the corner delicatessen last night—between ten and ten thirty, according to the owner—to buy coffee and milk for breakfast. The bag of groceries still sat on the kitchen counter where she had put it. For such a short trip, and on such a sultry night, she might very well not bother to close and lock the terrace window. They were checking for signs of such an intruder; unfortunately the thunderstorm that came later in the night had probably washed them away. The terrace was accessible from the roof via a drain pipe, and with no superintendent on the premises—he lived in the house down the street—and a street door that could be opened with a dime, it wouldn't be much of a trick for someone to get into the house and up on the roof. Again unfortunately, the fourth-floor tenants were away on vacation. Like the young man on the first floor; he had been due back last night, but his plane had been delayed by bad weather until this morning. So the only two people in the house had been Miss Baxter and Mrs. Klein, on the floor below her. Mrs. Klein reported hearing someone running down the stairs last night a few minutes after she came back from walking her dog. She couldn't be sure about the time. Ten thirty. Eleven. She hadn't thought to look at the clock. Nothing else out of the way. Just the footsteps. Very fast. Very hard. Bubbles had barked his head off. He was a wonderful watchdog; she never had to worry with him around. She hadn't heard Miss Baxter go out or come back, so the footsteps must have been after her trip to the delicatessen.

To make things even more difficult, there were no neighbors from across the street to observe last night's comings and goings. Almost the entire block opposite Enid's house was taken up by a grade school and a huge new apartment house in process of construction—both of course empty on a Sunday night in July.

Yes, a prowler was certainly a possibility. Though they couldn't rule out the other possibilities yet. Mrs. Nicholson hadn't heard from Miss Baxter or seen her over the week end?

"You mean do I have an alibi?" Hazel asked drily. "No, I didn't hear from Enid or see her over the week end. Last night my sister and I went to the movies to cool off. Got caught in the thunderstorm on our way home. Let's clear Rosemary while we're at it. She spent the week end with friends in Connecticut and came back to town this morning on the train. In case you're interested in names and addresses we can supply them."

"I'd appreciate it," said the detective blandly. "Thank you very much."

Later, when the lawyer called about Enid's will, she realized that checking the Nicholson alibis wasn't such a farfetched idea after all. Enid had been an only child; except for two cousins she had never seen there were no relatives. Her estate was divided between Hazel, who was named executrix of her will, and Rosemary. The amount of money involved was not large; still, people had been known to murder other people for far less. People who had been told the terms of other people's wills, that is. To Hazel and Rosemary the news of their inheritance—the detective could believe it or not—was a shock, a queerly sad jolt of discovery about Enid and the life they had imagined for her, the glittering, crowded social life. . .

A lonely sort of person. This time Hazel said it out loud. "Don't," croaked Rosemary, and fled to her bedroom.

Hazel herself would have liked a good cry. Instead, she pitched in and made the funeral arrangements.

And after that was over, there were other tasks. Enid's will contained a few specific bequests: her family silver went to the cousins, books and certain pieces of jewelry to friends, her clothes to her maid Carrie. It was left to Hazel to sort out and dispose of the rest—furniture, pictures, dishes, household equipment, all the accumulation of a woman's lifetime. The job, which she tackled with her usual forthright energy, was more time-consuming than she would have thought possible. Each session she spent in that old, high-ceilinged apartment seemed only to open up new pockets of possessions to be looked through and consigned to whatever fate she decided was appropriate.

On the Saturday after Enid's death she arrived bright and early, determined to finish up. Martin Shipley was mousing around in his little scrap of garden. "How about clearing out those books today?" she said briskly. They were his, according to the will, but so far he had put off moving them down to his place. Squeamish about going back to Enid's apartment, Hazel supposed. Well, she hadn't exactly relished the idea, either. But she had done it. "It won't take long, once you get at it. And it will be that much accomplished."

This time, rather to her surprise, he did not stall. "Yes. All right." He straightened up by degrees and wiped his hands along the sides of his faded dungarees. A scrawny, forlorn-looking specimen; once more Hazel wondered how he and Enid had happened to strike up a friendship. Probably a simple matter of propinquity.

But before the morning was over she changed her mind about Martin Shipley. In the first place, he turned out to be the kind of worker that Hazel's farmer father used to call a hustler. Instead of fading out of the picture, as he had every right to do once he had cleared out the books, he set to and helped her with the kitchen cupboards. She was inclined to dither over decisions. Not Martin. "Throw it out, it's no earthly use." "Give it to Carrie." "The Salvation Army." And that would be that. On to the next shelf.

He had a nice, quiet sense of humor, too. Little jokes sprang up between them. Now and then Hazel had to laugh, just at the sight of him up there on the step-stool: those long arms of his that seemed to angle out in all directions, the stretch of knobby backbone showing between his dungarees and t-shirt, his bony skull with the cowlick sticking up from the crown. There was something engaging about his very lack of grace or good looks. He wasn't all that unattractive, anyway, especially when he smiled; she pointed out to herself his high forehead and steady eyes.

There were one or two sombre moments. In the middle

of taking down the drapes he stopped and looked off into space. "I remember helping her put these up. She wasn't tall enough to manage by herself, even with the big ladder. . . Haven't the police turned up anything? Anything at all?"

"Not as far as I know," said Hazel. "They're still working on it, of course."

But the days had gone by, with no break in the case; the story had receded from glaring tabloid headlines to the back pages; and without realizing it until now, Hazel no longer expected a break. The chances of plucking, from all the swarming city, one anonymous prowler who had panicked and killed and run—too remote, too remote.

"They kept asking me about her friends. You too? Yeah." Martin peered down at her from the stepladder. "They had her address book. I don't know how many times they took me through it, name by name."

"I know. And most of them were just names to me. Didn't mean a thing. Except for the business contacts. You probably knew more about her social life than I did."

"Did you ever meet that friend of hers—what's-his-name?—Victor Holm? He's an architect, I think."

Hazel shook her head. "They asked about him. But his name doesn't ring any bells with me. Why?"

"She used to know him in Philadelphia. He's moved to New York now. I met him up here once—oh, it must have been two or three months ago. In the spring. His name was in her book, so I suppose they talked to him too. I suppose they went right down the list, checking everybody against everybody else."

"Probably." Hazel hadn't thought of it before. It made

her feel vaguely uncomfortable. "Well, apparently they didn't find any red-hot suspects. Or if they did they're keeping it awfully quiet."

"That's all they could do if they didn't have any proof," Martin said slowly. "Just bide their time and wait for the murderer to make a slip. The famous, fatal slip they all theoretically make."

"But I thought—I still think it was a prowler." She cleared her throat. "Just one of those senseless things, like being killed by a hit and run driver. As impersonal as that. All the details point to a prowler."

"They could point the other way too, though. If somebody she knew rang her doorbell she might let them in. It could have been like that. Not through the terrace at all." After a moment's silence he reached again for the curtain rod and wrenched it free of its moorings. "Look out below!" The drapes descended majestically, exuding dust. The subject was dropped.

Then there was the business about the ring. Enid had left to Martin, besides her books and anything he might want from the terrace, her jade ring. "I put it aside for you," Hazel told him. "Here. You might as well take it now."

"But that's not the one—" It came blurting out, apparently before he could stop it. He flushed.

"What do you mean it's not the one? I went through all her jewelry, and it's the only jade ring I found. Look for yourself, if you think I'm trying to hold out on you."

"Of course I don't think that!" It was a sign of how far their friendship had already progressed—the way they now glared at each other. "I expected it to be the other one, you know, the one she always wore. It was smaller than this one, and the setting was gold, not silver. Maybe three or four little squares of jade set in a row. She always wore it. Surely you remember it?"

Now that he mentioned it, yes. When Hazel closed her eyes she could see Enid's small, nervous hand, and on it the ring; she had had a habit of twisting it round and round with her thumb. "But where could it be? Honest and true, Martin, the lawyer and I sorted everything out, and this was the only. . . Unless she was buried with it still on. That's possible, I suppose."

That had to be it, she decided, after they had searched the apartment without success.

"It doesn't matter," Martin said. "This one will do just as well as a keepsake. Something to remember her by. That's all that matters. Not that I'm apt to forget her," he added, and his face was so stricken that Hazel's heart went out to him.

"There. No use brooding."

"She was my best friend," said Martin. "My only friend."

"Oh come on, now. A young fellow like you lonely?" she began. But then their eyes met, and she broke off, inwardly cringing at her own glib heartiness. At that moment he looked like the oldest man in the world, far too old to remember what hope or joy felt like. And lonely, lonely, in a way that was beyond Hazel's ken, except for this brief glimmer. Enid had known, though; she and Martin had been birds of a feather.

And yet when he smiled—as he was smiling now—he changed into the shy, rather unprepossessing, but likable lad she had spent the morning with. Could she have imagined that ancient, tragic mask of a moment ago? "I'm hungry," he said. "How about knocking off and coming down to my place for a sandwich?"

"Fine. The only thing is, Rosemary promised to come down and lend a hand. . . Well, I can leave her a note, can't I?"

Rosemary arrived as they were finishing their sandwiches and beginning a second round of beers. She and Martin, though they had both attended the funeral services for Enid, had not met formally until now. They eyed each other—Martin with open appreciation, Rosemary with the inscrutable expression she was cultivating this summer. She's so pretty, Hazel thought, with the familiar pang of pride, wistfulness and surprise. She had never been pretty herself; how had she happened to produce a daughter like this? Rosemary's light brown hair, with sun-bleached streaks in it, was hitched up on top today, exposing her neat little ears and the graceful line of her neck. Her nose was pert, her eyelashes extravagant, her dress pink-and-white striped, like a peppermint stick. Martin, poor boy, was obviously and acutely aware of his own sweaty, dust-streaked attire. Not to mention the state of his apartment, which was about what you would expect. Hazel, watching him stumble over his own feet as he cleared a chair for Rosemary, felt suddenly protective.

"Martin's been working like a dog up there all morning," she said. "Wait till you see what we've accomplished. He deserves a medal."

The smile Rosemary dispensed was abstracted. Either this was part of the inscrutable business or her thoughts really were otherwise engaged. Hazel had no idea which. Until a few minutes later, when Rosemary broke off in the middle of something else to exclaim, "Martin Shipley! I knew the name was familiar but I couldn't think where. . . Now I remember. Of course. I knew Bill Dunning at college, he used to date my roommate, and it was his sister—" Her face suddenly turned fiery red. "Forgive me. I'm so sorry. I shouldn't have mentioned it."

"Why not?" Into the well of silence Martin dropped the two words, small and hard as pebbles. He kept his eyes lowered. His whole body seemed to have locked and gone rigid. "Your roommate. His sister. And my wife. All very cozy."

"Your wife?" said Hazel. "I didn't know you were married!"

At that he did look up; his eyes were stony, his mouth set in a wolfish sort of smile. "Hard to believe, isn't it? I was married. I had a wife. Unfortunately, she died."

"I'm so sorry," Rosemary said again, helplessly, and he turned the wolfish smile on her. With one accord, she and Hazel stood up; Martin unlocked himself and rose, obviously as eager as they to end this uncomfortable little scene. There was no mention of his earlier offer to help with the final chores in Enid's apartment, nothing left of the comradeship that had sprung up between him and Hazel. The few perfunctory words of thanks she mumbled embarrassed them both; they did not even shake hands. But when she looked back, halfway up the first flight of stairs, he was still standing there in the doorway, watching them, with such a hungry expression on his face. Like a stray dog, she thought, and she might have turned back if he had not stepped inside just then and slammed the door.

"What was all that about?" she demanded when she caught up with Rosemary outside Enid's door.

"Joyce Dunning. He was married to Joyce Dunning!

And to think I blurted it out like that, why, I could have sunk through the floor! You must have read about it in the papers, Mom, her family carried on like crazy."

"When she married Martin, you mean?"

"Of course not when she married him. When she was killed in that accident. Surely I must have told you— No, maybe not. It was three years ago, the summer you were out in California, and I suppose by the time I saw you again the whole thing had simmered down. I got in on it on account of Penny, she was mad for Bill Dunning at that point, so naturally she was all agog. . ." They were in Enid's living room now; facing each other—Hazel open-mouthed, Rosemary aware of the effect she was producing. "They suspected foul play, you see. Her family. They tried to get him arrested for murder."

"Martin? They accused Martin of murdering his wife?"

"Well, he could have pushed her," said Rosemary calmly. "He was with her at this quarry when it happened. This old abandoned quarry. He and Joyce were visiting her folks in the country, Massachusetts, I think, and they'd just had a fight. So she went tearing out of the house, and he followed her, and somehow or other she slipped and fell. Broke her neck. Her father screamed his head off to the police, and I don't know whether they decided Martin was telling the truth, or whether they just figured they'd never be able to prove he wasn't. Anyway, they didn't arrest him."

"I should think not," said Hazel, in a voice so much louder and more emphatic than she had intended that it startled her. "I can't imagine anybody looking or acting less like a murderer than that boy. Can you?"

Rosemary's answer was slow in coming. She inspected her pale pink fingernails. "No. But then— Well, who knows what a murderer's supposed to look like? I certainly don't. I've never met one personally. As far as I know."

Suddenly Hazel shivered.

chapter 4

So much for the Nicholsons, Martin thought as he slammed the door on them. He grinned to himself, imagining the lurid tale Rosemary was no doubt already pouring out, to the accompaniment of shocked gasps from her mother. And he seemed like such a nice boy, she would repeat at intervals. Past tense. Seemed. The word itself held overtones of fraudulence. Now that she knew what lay behind his false front, she would remember one or two odd moments. Not so much what he said, she would explain, as the way he said it. He couldn't, of course, have had anything to do with what had happened to Enid; but all the same it was strange, first the business about his wife, and now this.

Yes. Very strange. Almost too much of a coincidence. Oh, he could hear them, he could see the frightened flutter of Rosemary's eyelashes, the glaze of dismay settling on Hazel's plain, forthright face.

And they didn't know the half of it. Victor Holm was

just a name to them. Enid had spared them her confidences; she had extracted no promise from them. He could almost hate her for the shrewd instinct that had guided her straight to him: the one person she could trust to keep that promise. Once again he toyed with the notion of breaking it. He saw himself marching into the police station, upright citizen that he was, belatedly volunteering the information he had hitherto withheld, explaining in manly ringing tones that on second thought he had decided to put public duty before his personal code of honor. Justice must be served. Yea, yea. Murder must be avenged.

But they must already have checked on Vic, along with everyone else whose name was listed in Enid's address book. Checked and cleared him. Or perhaps not cleared him; they might still be watching and waiting, quietly probing for weak spots in his story. They certainly didn't have to depend on Martin to tell them about the affair between Enid and Vic four years ago; it had been pretty generally known in Philadelphia. As far as its resumption was concerned—well, they didn't need Martin there, either. That was their business, to put two and two together and come up with at least four, more likely five. Vic himself might very well have admitted it. Why not, if he had a good enough alibi for the Sunday night of her death? And if it was all that good, Martin's little tattled tidbits weren't going to break it. There was no guarantee the police would believe him, anyway. Just his word for it, the word of a fellow with a mighty peculiar history of his own. . .

That, of course, was the crux of the matter, the one angle that made him incapable of breaking his promise to Enid. Because he knew what it was to be accused without proof, he could not point his finger at Vic, at least not at this stage, with nothing more substantial to go on than the memory of Enid's morbid fancies, brandy-induced. Her voice came back to him: "I just mentioned the possibility. Very remote. And anyway, it would be my own fault, for needling him into it."

Definitely not at this stage. But not ever? Never? Supposing he were to come across some solid evidence of Vic's guilt, would he take it to the police? Or would he find some further excuse for not speaking out? With his talent for rationalization, he wouldn't have much trouble. After all, it meant not only breaking his word to Enid, it meant aligning himself on the side of a group he had come to regard, thanks to Joyce's family, as his natural enemies. The sight of a cop could still make him flinch.

Curiosity spread in him like an itch. In addition to his own unpredictable reactions, there was the swarm of questions about Vic: his thoughts and feelings, whatever they might be; how much of them he could hide or not hide; what part of the truth he had dared to tell the police, what part his wife.

He sat down. Absent-mindedly he sipped the remains of Hazel's beer. (They had stood not upon the order of their going.) Yes. He was itching to see Vic. He had a right to investigate the matter on a strictly private basis and settle it in his own mind. That would not be betraying Enid's trust in him. Time enough later to decide about the police.

But he couldn't just barge in and start asking questions as if he were a cop. Victor Holm was no man to stand for any such nonsense. In fact, Martin wondered if he was a match for Vic, whatever tactics he might adopt. A very cagey customer. Still, he had nothing to lose by trying.

Surely he could invent some pretext, some plausible reason for calling Vic. . .

His eye fell on the pile of books from Enid's apartment, which he had dumped on the floor. A helter-skelter assortment: current novels, Shakespeare, books on gardening, interior decorating, furniture, architecture. Architecture. He plucked one at random; Vic's name sprang at him from the flyleaf.

Five minutes later he was speaking his piece to Vic over the telephone. "Martin Shipley. You may not remember me, but we met once some time ago at Enid—"

"Yes, of course. I've been meaning to call you. I don't know any of Enid's other friends here in New York, and I'd like to talk to you. How about coming over? We're only a couple of blocks away, you know."

"Yes, I know." Thrown off his stride, Martin floundered on. "What I called about, Enid's books, I found several of yours among them, and I thought you might want—"

"What? Sorry, I can't hear you."

Martin went through it again, this time slowly and distinctly. Vic disposed of it in short order. "No, I don't want them back. Thanks anyway. I'd forgotten she had them. If you're not busy this afternoon, drop in for a drink. Any time that suits you. You've got the address?"

Just like that it was settled. He had geared himself for talking to Vic alone. The unknown quantity of Vic's wife both alarmed and intrigued him. But somehow the whole business had been taken out of his hands: a trial sample of Vic's oneupmanship. Where Martin had made his mistake—he decided while he showered and changed his clothes—was in laying out too rigid a plan for himself ahead of time, with no allowance for unforeseeable contingencies. From now on he would play it by ear. He could hardly do anything else, with the performance taking place on Vic's home grounds, very likely with his wife as audience. Thelma. His only source of information on the subject of Thelma was Enid, the barbed comments she had now and then let fly. He knew better than to take them as gospel truth.

Was Thelma supposed to act as a deterrent to Martin? Was that why Vic had avoided a tête-à-tête, because he was counting on her, just the fact of her presence, to keep the conversation within the limits of safety and decorum? The nerve of him! For all he knew, Martin might be loaded with bombshells, with no scruples about dropping them, never mind who might be around. It was galling, to be dismissed as no more of a menace than that.

He was a little startled when he reached the address on Third Avenue: instead of a regular apartment house, it was an old four-story building, jammed in between taller, newer neighbors. The first two floors were occupied by a surgical appliance store and its stock room; the Holms had the top half of the place to themselves. A narrow staircase led to their apartment, which no doubt had great possibilities, as yet unrealized. The big living room into which Vic ushered him—still with that brisk cordiality, quite a change from their previous encounter—had an unsettled look, as if all the furniture were just as the moving men had left it. But Martin's impression of the room and its decor was fleeting; it was the people in it that riveted his attention. There were two women, instead of the one he had been prepared for. Two women, and he didn't know which was Thelma, and he had never been easy about meeting strangers. He felt himself breaking into a nervous sweat.

It turned out that Thelma was the tall one with the bangs. "Lulu and I are about to leave for a matinee. Do forgive us, won't you. And I'm sorry we're still in such a shambles. It's going to be beautiful. We hope." She crossed the room with her hand thrust out: like a child running to meet him, Martin thought, a friendly child who took it for granted she was going to like and be liked. There was a quality of headlong warmth about her that made her seem vulnerable. Dangerously so, from Martin's point of view; she might very well have acted as a deterrent. Thank God for the matinee. She was nothing at all like Enid. (Well, why should he have expected her to be?) None of Enid's miniature delicacy, none of her chic, none of her sleek darkness. All the same, a real rival—as Enid had been the first to recognize. When Thelma smiled, the imperfections of her face, with its overlarge mouth and slightly crooked teeth, were somehow transformed into assets. Really, it was quite a magical smile; you smiled back, whether you meant to or not.

Lulu was an expensive-looking item, polished and tinted and brushed to a high gloss. She had a husky voice, a compact figure, and a coolly appraising, humorous eye. Nothing vulnerable about her. Her last name was McGrath. Mrs. McGrath. A friend of the Holms from Philadelphia. She too had known Enid—well, not really known her, but they had met now and then at parties. Poor girl, what a shocking thing. Dreadful.

"I think Vic said you were a neighbor of Enid's?" said Thelma. "In the same house?"

"Yes. I have the ground-floor apartment." Martin hardened his heart and went on. "We saw quite a bit of each other. That's where I met Mr. Holm, in fact, one evening in Enid's apartment." A small bombshell, perhaps? She was no longer looking at him.

"Remember, Thelma?" said Vic. "It wasn't long after we ran into Enid at that press party. She asked me then if I'd take a look at a job she was working on and tell her what I thought."

Loyally, obediently, Thelma's head bobbed up and down. "So I suppose you had a session with the police too, Mr. Shipley. The same as we did."

"We certainly did," Lulu said. "I was here that week end, too—I sneak off to New York whenever Vic and Thelma will put up with me—and I was just leaving to catch the train back home Monday morning, when here came the cops. What a business! They phoned Vic at the office and got him back here, to double-check Thelma and me, I suppose. Not that they weren't perfectly nice about everything. And after all, that's their job, asking questions. How else are they going to come up with the right answer?"

"They haven't come up with any kind of an answer so far," Martin pointed out. "Maybe they haven't asked the right questions."

"I can't think of any they missed." Thelma laughed tremulously. "Personally I felt as if I'd been put through the wringer and hung out to dry. Not just once, either. They've been back a couple of times, just to see if we remembered anything else. And they've given Lulu the same treatment. We've all three been grilled to a turn, individually and collectively. . .Vic dear, fix Mr. Shipley a drink. He can have some of my ginger ale if he's on the wagon, poor soul." She made a funny face at Martin.

"You're not, are you? Nobody is but me. We've got to run. So sorry. Do come again."

"See you later. Behave yourselves now." Vic kissed her, and over her shoulder exchanged a meaningful glance with Lulu. "Don't worry, I'm in good hands," said Thelma rather irritably. Something of a lush, Enid had reported. Could be. And Lulu's role was to keep her in line? Could be, Martin repeated to himself, and sat down on the couch while Vic got busy at the bar with gin and tonic.

It really was quite a living room. Except for the kitchen alcove, it took up the whole floor. The walls were of whitewashed brick, spectacularly bare and high. At one end an open stairway curved upward, presumably to the bedrooms. There was a handsome Oriental rug on the floor, but no pictures or books. Even Martin, who had little interest in such matters, realized that it lacked the finishing touches.

He had decided on a blunt approach. He would wait till Vic mixed the drinks and sat down. Then he would come out with it: You wanted to talk to me about Enid?

But again Vic beat him to the draw. "What's your theory about Enid?" he asked as he handed Martin his glass.

"My theory?"

"Sure, your theory. Who's in a better position to have one? Knowing her as well as you did. Living in the same house."

"Okay, but I wasn't there the night it happened." Why should he sound so defensive, damn it? And don't think Vic wasn't enjoying it: barely able to keep from smirking. "I wasn't even in town. I was on vacation."

"That's right. I remember now, the police mentioned the house was practically empty. Nobody there but one other woman tenant. And Enid. And of course whoever did it. When did you get back from your vacation?" A nice sociable question. Vic tacked it on as if it were an afterthought.

"Didn't the police tell you that, too? Monday morning. I was due back Sunday night, but the plane was held up on account of weather. So you know as much as I do about what went on. At least you were here in town. Or so I gather."

"Oh yes. I was here all right. We went to the beach in the afternoon, Thelma and Lulu and I, and I folded up early, right after dinner. Sun affects me that way." Vic sat down and crossed his legs, triumphantly at ease. Well, it was an alibi of sorts. The police must have bought it. No reason why they shouldn't. Even if Martin had chosen to talk, it might not have made any difference. He could see Vic—open-faced, obviously a man of substance with nothing to hide—looking the police in the eye as he answered their questions in his deep, assured voice. Yes. Trust Vic to strike the right note. And Thelma to back him up. "All right. Leaving Sunday night out of it," he was going on now to Martin, "I thought you might have a line on what led up to it. I mean, in case the police are wrong and it wasn't a prowler. I was counting on you to know about her friends here in New York. Or her enemies. Anyway, the people she was seeing."

"I know she was seeing you," said Martin. "Whether your wife knows it or not."

He had the satisfaction of seeing Vic's face turn red. "I had that coming, I guess. Don't bother telling me what you think of me. I agree. I'm sorry about Thelma. I always was. A hell of a lot of good that does. Being sorry. I don't expect you to understand. If you'd ever been married—"

"As it happens, I have been. Didn't Enid tell you?" (But of course she hadn't. His confidences had been safe with her. As hers were with him.)

"She told me nothing about you," said Vic bitterly. "For all I know you were in love with her too."

Martin sipped his drink contentedly. It was pleasant to have the upper hand, for a change. "I don't think you had any real competition. Judging from the way she talked to me. She used to go out with other men now and then, but not after you turned up."

"So she talked about me, did she? It figures. Good Neighbor Martin. Always ready with the valuable free advice."

"None that she ever took," said Martin. "And whatever she told me, I didn't pass it on to the police. If that's what's eating on you."

"What's eating on me is that she's dead!" Vic turned on him savagely. "Dead, God damn it. I've lost her, I'll never see her again. My girl. Gone. Dead. Can't you understand anything?"

Martin had a sudden strong urge to yell back exactly how much he understood, and exactly why: Joyce too was dead, he too had lost his girl, they had suspected him—as he suspected Vic—of killing her, and with as much reason. He clenched his teeth against the words. What if he and Vic did happen to share a similar set of circumstances? That didn't make them soul mates. It was preposterous that he should feel so much as a second's rapport with this violent, jealous, bullying fellow. This murderer. Even Enid, who had once loved him, had recognized him as a menace. And Martin had seen for himself how full of tricks he was, what a manipulator.

"I understand plenty," he said. "She was the best friend I ever had. You can take that any way you want to. I know what it means, and so did she. If you were so damn much in love with her, why didn't you hang on to her when you had her, back there in Philadelphia?"

"Because I never do anything right! You got any more bright questions?"

They glared at each other in silence. Finally Martin said (because he was a little ashamed of himself, but not about to admit it), "You know, Enid once said the same thing to me. That she never did the right thing except at the wrong moment."

"She did?" Vic scanned his face hungrily. "Well, it was the truth. She had a way of belting you with things just when you were in no shape to take them. . . We fought like hell. Did she tell you that? And yet—we were happy. You're right, I shouldn't have let her go. It was a long time sinking in. But I've known for a year now that nothing was ever going to be any good without her. That's why I came to New York. I figured we'd run into each other, sooner or later. It had to be chance. Don't ask me who made the rules, but I wasn't allowed to call her. Sounds nutty, doesn't it? Like a superstition. If I tried to push fate I'd bollix everything up. You know?"

Martin nodded curtly. It had been the same with him and Joyce. The rigid tabus. The signs and portents: colors, for instance, he had always had the conviction that green was the color of disaster for them, long before that last night when she stormed out in her green dress. They too had fought like hell. And been happy. But then so had many another set of lovers. If Vic had any notions about working on his sympathies. . .

Could he have sensed, in some uncanny way, that tiny flicker of rapport between them and be trying now to fan it into a nice comfortable blaze for his own protection? It was impossible to tell. His face, for all its surface candor, was inscrutable; his hazy gray eyes seemed fixed on some private horizon.

"Didn't it ever occur to you that she might have changed her mind about you?" Martin asked. "After all, a lot can happen in four years. What made you think she was going to give you a second chance?"

"Because I couldn't stand it if she didn't," said Vic defiantly. The egotist's answer: I want it so, therefore it is so. "You've got to believe in something. All right. I believed in us. Enid and me. And I was right. The only difference was that this time around we weren't settling for what we had before." He banged his glass down. His voice grew louder, even more defiant. "We were getting married as soon as—as soon as possible."

"I see," said Martin. It wasn't the way he had heard it from Enid. More than two months ago, true; but since then she had mentioned Vic often, without ever once hinting at any such drastic switch in plans. Martin would have known if she had been dissembling—and anyway, why should she? As for the gap of ten days while he was away on vacation, she had written him once, a chatty little letter about inconsequentials. No. He simply did not believe in this projected, over-emphasized marriage. Vic was lying—possibly because he was an egotist incapable of facing the unacceptable truth, possibly because he was a murderer bent on covering up his motive. Possibly both. "Do the police know all this?"

"They know we had an affair four years ago. And that we'd met again here in New York. But not about our plans. You see, Thelma—"

Martin finished it for him. "You hadn't broken it to her yet. And she hadn't guessed?"

"I doubt it. In fact, I'd be willing to bet on it. Thelma's like that. Inclined to dodge reality." She wasn't the only one, but Martin managed not to say it. "If she guessed anything at all, it was just—well, Philadelphia all over again. Which was bad enough, God knows. I told you before, I'm not proud of myself when it comes to Thelma."

"She's a charming woman," said Martin carefully.

"Very charming. Especially when she's on the wagon. No need to beat about the bush. Enid must have told you. Probably laid it on too thick, in fact. Thelma's sometimes a problem drinker, but that doesn't mean. . . Lulu's taken her on as one of her rehabilitation projects. She loves sticking people together again. Or trying to. It doesn't always work, of course."

"Not always with Thelma, you mean?"

"So far so good. Let's hope. One thing about Lulu, she doesn't give up easy. She'd still be spoon-feeding that worthless brother of hers if her husband hadn't put his foot down. He's one of The McGraths, Main Line, plenty of dough. Lulu was a hat check girl when he married her. So he calls the turns. Anyway, you can see why I held off telling Thelma."

"Yes. I suppose you'll never tell her now."

"Not much point to it. Not much point to anything, if you ask me." He fumbled with his glass. His face looked empty. Bereft. "Except I'd like to get the guy that did it."

"So would I," said Martin. "Not that it would bring her back. But I'd just like to know. . . When was the last time you saw her? It must have been after I did."

"Thursday. The Thursday night before it happened. We had dinner at her place. She didn't seem worried about anything, if that's what you're getting at."

You wouldn't know it if she was, Martin thought. Impervious bastard. And if that happened to be one of the nights when you fought like hell, you'd certainly keep it to yourself.

"She mentioned you," Vic added, grudgingly. "Said she missed you. You say she left you her books? In her will?"

"Her books and her jade ring." Martin straightened up; he had forgotten about the ring until now. "Only the ring seems to be missing. Anyway, Mrs. Nicholson and I couldn't find it. There was another one, but not the one she always wore—"

"I know. I ought to. I gave it to her."

"Yes. Well, I assumed that was the one she meant for me to have. But it's gone. We looked through everything. It's the only thing in the way of a clue I can offer. And a pretty damn thin one. Would a prowler take it and nothing else, not even her watch or her wallet? Maybe. If something scared him off before he had time. . . On the other hand, Mrs. Nicholson may be right and she was buried with it still on her finger."

Vic opened his mouth and closed it again. For what was surely a whole minute, he sat very still. Then he said softly, "I hope she was. I wouldn't want anybody else to have it. And that goes for you too, bud," he added, with a sudden, disarming smile.

"I don't blame you," said Martin before he could stop himself. He stood up. He'd better get out of here quick, before he lost his grip entirely and started telling Vic the story of his life. Enid had been right: this man was dangerous.

chapter 5

"I hope you don't mind my ringing your bell," Rosemary said, as she had planned in advance. "I happened to be in the neighborhood, and I just thought I'd stop by and see if you were home."

There was a noticeable silence before Martin—who was not behaving at all as she had planned—said, "Okay. I'm home."

"So I see." She produced a tinny, solitary laugh. "Don't let me interrupt you if you're busy."

"I'm not," he said. He did not open the door any wider. On the other hand, he did not close it.

"Well, if you're not even going to ask me in—"

"By all means." He gestured sweepingly. "I assumed you'd be scared to come in. How do you know you're not taking your life in your hands?"

"Don't be silly," she said, and stepped past him into the dusky living room. It had been slicked up since Saturday, but it still wasn't cheery. He couldn't have been reading;

there wasn't enough light. Had he just been sitting here staring into space? "Look, I'm sorry about the other day. I didn't do it on purpose. I'm just stupid. If that makes any difference."

Personally, she thought it was quite a handsome apology. Martin ignored it. "How's your mother? I bet she doesn't know you're here." He stood beside her, exuding hostility. But misery too; she saw that when he switched on the lamp. "It must have given her quite a turn to find out this isn't the first mysterious death I've been mixed up in. Well? Didn't it?"

"I told you I'm sorry." She was conscious of an unpleasant little inner voice: Yes, and you thought that would fix everything, didn't you? Thought all you had to do was flutter the eyelashes and tremble the lip and he'd be eating out of your hand. And now it turns out you're not so irresistible, your nose is out of joint. "After all, it's no deep dark secret about Joyce. Plenty of people besides me know it. It would almost certainly have come out, one way or another."

"That's what I figured, with my usual low cunning. That's why I told the police myself, when they first asked me about Enid. As I expect you discovered when you went panting to them with the news."

"I did not!" she cried. "And neither did my mother, and neither of us ever will."

"Very kind of you, I'm sure. But doesn't it bother you, the possibility that you may be obstructing justice?"

"Oh, what's the use of trying to talk to you? You're impossible! Absolutely impossible!" She spun around and made for the door.

"Don't go," he said unwillingly. But urgently. "Please. Don't go, Rosemary." His hand touched her arm—for a moment only; she drew back instantly and stood still, in complete astonishment. So this was what had brought her back to his apartment. Not curiosity or a wish to apologize, but simply this, the good old basic drawing power that kept the human race in business. (Rosemary had no trouble recognizing it, in spite of her somewhat limited experience.) Never mind that he wasn't what she thought of as her type—that knobby, unhappy face; the personality that, beyond touchiness and a gift for sarcasm, was an unknown quantity to her. The spot on her arm still glowed and tingled.

"Stay and talk to me," he said. "Or— How about dinner?"

"I've already eaten."

"Yeah. Me too. A drink, then? Or coffee?"

"Coffee would be nice." She sat down, demurely smoothing her skirt, demurely lowering her eyelashes. Now that the first shock of surprise was past, she felt rather smug: at least the reaction seemed to be a mutual one, not all on her side.

The coffee was strong, the cups chipped, the sugar bowl on the sticky side. After a minute or two of awkward small talk, Martin said bruskly, "I don't see what's so impossible about assuming you'd go to the police. Seems perfectly logical to me."

"Well, it doesn't to me. What's the point in dragging up past history that's got nothing to do with Enid?"

"You'll have to admit it's an interesting coincidence, though. The police certainly thought so. A very interesting coincidence. Yes indeed. They'd have had quite a case against me, if it hadn't been for my dear little alibi."

"Without a motive? That's ridiculous. You had no earthly reason for killing Enid."

"How do you know? We could have gotten into a violent quarrel about—about horticulture. Anything. And I have this ungovernable temper. Just ask your friend Bill Dunning. He can tell you. He knows more about the quarrels Joyce and I had than I do myself. Especially the last one. He quoted it verbatim."

He was giving her the ferocious smile. She remembered it from Saturday. "Past history," she repeated doggedly. "It's no good brooding about it. All right. The Dunnings gave you a hard time. But they didn't get anywhere with accusing you of—of what happened to Joyce. The police didn't buy their story. They bought yours. You were cleared. It was three years ago, and it's finished, and the only thing to do now is forget it."

"I should forget it. How about you? You were the one that started all this."

She flushed. "And you're never going to forgive me for it, are you? You're going to hoard it up along with everything the Dunnings said. Another wound to lick."

"I forgive you," he said stiffly. "If it hadn't been you, it would have been somebody else. That's the thing, you see. I never know when it's going to happen again, I just know it will, sooner or later. It's not very—tranquilizing."

No, it wouldn't be. Rosemary could see that. "But it doesn't have to spoil your whole *life!* So somebody sees you or hears your name and says, 'Aren't you the Martin Shipley that et cetera.' So you say, 'Yes. Have you read any good books lately?' And that's that."

"God, you're wholesome," he said. "I find it simpler to avoid people whenever possible."

"Then why did you ask me to stay? You didn't have to."

"You didn't have to ring my bell, either. But I'm glad

you did." He laughed. Really laughed. "I didn't start out as a hermit. It's just a form of protective coloration. I'm a self-made neurotic. That's what Enid used to call me."

"About Enid." Rosemary took a sip of coffee and went on rather nervously, "My mother may go to the police again. Not on account of you. Not that at all. But Enid's jade ring, to tell them it's missing. If it really is. I mean—"

"It is. You can tell her not to bother. I went back to them myself yesterday, so they already know. It wasn't buried with her."

"What did the police say? Do they think it's important?"

"Who knows? They didn't discuss the fine points of the case with me. She might have lost it, of course. Or, if it was a prowler who killed her, he might have stolen it. It wasn't particularly valuable, but. . . Did you ever meet Vic Holm? He's the fellow who gave it to her."

Rosemary shook her head. "Do you know him?"

"I met him once at Enid's, a couple of months ago. And the other day he asked me over for a drink. Enid had some of his books. That's why I called him. I don't really know him, no. Not of my own knowledge, as they say."

"What do you mean by that?"

"Enid used to talk about him now and then. They had quite a thing going at one time. But he was married—still is—so it sort of died on the vine." He looked at her sidewise. "Don't start getting ideas about Vic Holm. It's a waste of time. He's got an alibi too. Like me. Like everybody."

"Oh," she said, deflated. For she had started getting ideas: if only because of what seemed to her an oddly tentative note in Martin's voice. "Well, then, his wife. . ."

"I said everybody. And they don't just alibi each other, either. They had a guest that week end. The cops checked with her, too. Mrs. Lulu McGrath from Philadelphia. The three of them went to the beach Sunday afternoon, came back to the Holms' apartment, and spent a quiet evening there. One of them might be lying. Or even two. But three? It's just one too many."

"If she's a good enough friend of theirs, I suppose she might back them up," Rosemary said halfheartedly. "Or maybe they bribed her."

"She's rich. Her husband's one of The McGraths. I met her briefly—she was here again last week end—and she certainly didn't strike me as the type to carry friendship that far. After all, most people draw the line at murder. Judging by my own experience."

Brooding again, thought Rosemary; he would get no encouragement from her. "What are they like?" she asked. "The Holms?"

The telephone rang before he could tell her. Rosemary leafed through one of the magazines from the rack beside her to indicate that she was not listening; and listened for all she was worth. Nothing else to do, with the telephone right there on the table. She could even catch enough of the caller's mechanized voice to identify it as feminine. And voluble. Crackle, crackle, crackle.

"Oh yes," Martin said. "So that's where I left it. . . Well. . . If you're sure it's no bother. . . No, of course not. Awfully nice of you. . ." He hung up and cocked his head at Rosemary. "Stick around a few minutes and you'll see for yourself what one of the Holms is like. That was Vic's wife. Thelma. I forgot my lighter at their place the other day, and she's going to drop in and return it.

C

Seems she'll be passing right by here, on her way somewhere else."

"Then maybe I'd better go," said Rosemary, and stood up.

It brought him (as she had hoped?) leaping to his feet. "No! You can't go!" he cried. This time his hand stayed on her arm. Glowing. Tingling. "Why in the hell should you go?"

"Well. In case you want to talk to her alone or something." There was no time to give him the inscrutable look or flutter the eyelashes. Even if she had remembered. The kiss intervened.

Then they sat down again and exchanged nervous little pleasantries while they waited for the doorbell to ring.

Thelma Holm came in talking, in a bubbly, cheerful voice that made Rosemary think of a fountain. A slapdash sort of woman: she looked as if she had thrown on her clothes, run a comb through her bangs, dabbed on some lipstick, and rushed out without more than a glance in the mirror. And none of it mattered when she smiled.

"You should have told me you had company, Martin. I didn't mean to intrude." Her hand reached out impetuously for Rosemary's. "So nice to meet you. No, really, I mustn't stay. . . Well, just a minute then, if you're sure, let me see if I can unearth your lighter. . ." She sat down and began rummaging in her purse. "Oh dear, I hope it hasn't sunk to the bottom. Never to reappear."

"Would you like a cup of coffee while you're digging?" Martin asked. "Or can I fix you a drink?"

She hesitated. "I'd love one," she said sadly. "But I'm still on this abstemious kick. Better make it coffee. That's the trouble, you see, it's never just one with me. I get carried away. Ah, here we are." She produced the lighter with a flourish. "It's very strange, I never used to be a problem drinker. That's what Lulu and Vic call it. Not a drunk. Not even an alcoholic. A problem drinker. I guess it does sound more genteel. Whatever it is, I'm tired of being it. Do you suppose I'll ever get off the wagon and back to civilization?"

"Why not?" said Martin. "Lots of people do."

"I know. Vic did. My husband," she explained, turning her clear, dark-blue gaze in Rosemary's direction. Apparently she had no more reserve than a child; it was as if she already accepted them, without question, as old family friends instead of the bare acquaintances they actually were. "He drank himself practically into the gutter at one point. Years ago. No sugar, thank you, dear. It gives me the shudders even now to think of it. What we both went through, before he pulled himself together and got back on the beam. That's what's so strange, that now I should be the one. . . But then it fits in with this theory I have about myself." She paused, showing for the first time a trace of self-consciousness.

"Theory?" Rosemary prompted her.

"It's sort of balmy. All the same, it's been happening all my life. I seem to take on other people's afflictions. People that are close to me, I mean. My mother's asthma when I was little. Later on, my brother's bronchitis. My girl friend's low blood pressure. Vic and the drinking. He quit and after a while I started. As if I'd drawn it out of him. . . Does it sound too, too balmy?"

Uncertainly, eagerly, she scanned their faces, waiting for her cue, ready to play it whichever way they took it—seriously or as a joke. It was impossible to tell whether she sincerely believed in her "theory" or was merely trotting it out as a conversation piece. Rosemary had the feeling that Thelma herself did not know. And if she was this susceptible to other people's reactions (even people she hardly knew), then why shouldn't she be a pushover for the illnesses of those who were really close to her? Not so balmy after all, thought Rosemary, and wondered if Martin thought so too.

"It's an interesting angle," he was saying cautiously. "The asthma makes sense, because it's one of those suspicious diseases anyway. Easy enough for an impressionable child to pick it up from somebody she loved."

"I didn't say loved. I said close to. As a matter of fact, my mother and I hated each other. We were ahead of our time. It wasn't fashionable then." Her laugh pealed out. Then she added hastily, "Vic, of course. . . I don't hate Vic. With my mother I might have been just grabbing the spotlight because I couldn't bear for her to have it. But not with Vic. How could it be that, when he's all right now, and has been for years?"

All right as far as drinking was concerned. And if the affair with Enid had died on the vine, to use Martin's phrase— But he had also mentioned meeting Vic at Enid's apartment a couple of months ago. So they must have been seeing each other again. That didn't mean an affair, of course. Even so, thought Rosemary, it wouldn't make Vic's wife jump for joy. Might well edge her into the fuzzy realm of problem drinking, whether or not she already had a predilection for absorbing the afflictions of people she loved, hated, was close to. . .

"Delayed reaction, maybe," said Martin. "Or maybe it's got no connection with the fact that Vic used to drink too much. You could have hit the bottle for some entirely different reason."

She thought this over. Then she said matter-of-factly, "I suppose you mean Enid. But that was four years ago. Another one of your delayed. . . Oh! Now I remember. You met Vic at her apartment, didn't you, the night he stopped in to help her with that job, so you're assuming he'd taken up with her again here in New York. That's it, isn't it?"

"It did cross my mind," Martin admitted drily.

"Naturally. Considering how attractive Enid was." She turned toward Rosemary with an air of bright apology. "Poor dear, you're probably wondering what this is all about. Did you know her? Enid Baxter?"

"I knew her. She and my mother were in business together."

"Oh, of course. Nicholson. I don't know why it didn't register with me before now. Well, then, no need to explain to you why Martin made the mistake of assuming. . ." After a moment's silence she added wistfully, "I couldn't really blame Vic. She was so stunning. And brainy besides. I used to think if he left me—well, at least it wouldn't be for somebody humiliating. That was another bad time, but we got through it too. He didn't leave me, and Enid moved to New York, and that was the end of it."

Martin shifted uneasily in his chair. He was careful not to look at her. Finally he said, "And now she's dead. Yes. It's all over now." Which was not quite the same, thought Rosemary. "Vic and I talked about her the other day, you know, after you and Lulu left for the theater."

"I know. That is, I took it for granted you would. It's made it harder for Vic, not to have anyone to talk to. He can't very well, with me. Or thinks he can't. I wish he would, you know, it isn't healthy to bottle things up. Is it?"

"It all depends," said Martin, without specifying on what. "He seemed—very much upset about Enid."

"Of course. Who wouldn't be? Even if she had been only a speaking acquaintance. . . And then to hear it like that, from the police. And all the questions they asked. It was a nightmare. At least Vic wasn't hung over that morning, the way I was."

"Oh?"

"Yes. Oh." She gave a reminiscent groan. "Didn't Vic tell you how stoned I got the night before? The day before, actually. I started early, while we were at the beach, and didn't stop till I passed out on the living room couch. By then Vic had gone to bed, so poor Lulu was the one that got stuck with me."

"No, he didn't tell me."

"Chivalry or something. Well, we didn't go into every last sordid detail with the police, either. No point to it. After all, a lady's hangover is her own business. I should have thought the one I had that morning would be visible to the naked eye, but apparently not. Ah, the good old days. I haven't had a drink since." She jumped up and held out a hand to each of them. "I must go now, I didn't mean to stay this long. Thank you for the coffee—and the company. I do hope you'll call and come over some time soon, both of you. We don't know many people here yet, and Vic's been working overtime a lot, so. . ."

When he had closed the door behind her, Martin leaned against it, peering at Rosemary. "Well?"

"She's certainly an uninhibited type. I liked her, of course. Nobody could help it."

"Enid could."

"That's different. Enid— She *was* involved again with Vic, wasn't she?"

"According to Vic, very much so."

"You mean he told you? He must be as uninhibited as Thelma."

"Oh no, he isn't. Not by a long shot." Martin crossed slowly to his chair and sat down on the edge of it. "But he figured I already had a pretty good idea of what was going on, from Enid. It wasn't safe to deny it to me. Don't worry, Vic knows what to bottle up and what not to."

"You're making him sound like a real foul ball. Doesn't he have anything to recommend him?"

"Plenty. Too much. I liked him in spite of myself. But I— Well, let's put it this way. I don't have Thelma's unquestioning trust in him."

"I wonder," said Rosemary thoughtfully. "I know what they say, the wife's the last to find out. But in this case it's the second time around. Thelma could know more than she's letting on. It would explain why she turned into a lush."

But Martin shook his head. "She had already done that before Enid and Vic ran into each other again. Enid told me. Anyway, if she knows, why would she pretend not to?"

"Pride," Rosemary said promptly. "And loyalty to Vic. If the reporters had gotten hold of this angle, when Enid was killed, they'd have had a field day with it. I don't know how much Vic told the police—"

"As little as possible. You can be sure of that."

"Why are you so snide about him? After all, *you* didn't tell them about the affair, either."

"No," said Martin. He closed his eyes. "I had my reasons, as Vic had his. And Thelma hers—either because she didn't know or because she wanted to protect Vic."

"She was protecting herself too," Rosemary pointed out. "If you want to get technical—as well as snide—Thelma's the one with the best motive for wanting Enid out of the way."

"Thelma? Not Vic?"

"Of course not Vic. If he was in love with her—"

"He was. That much I believe."

"Well then, why would he want to kill her?"

"Why indeed?" He began to laugh, in an almost soundless, secret, infuriating way. "Okay, okay, I'm sorry. It's all academic, anyway, isn't it? Motive or no motive, neither of them could have killed her. Thelma was stoned, and Vic was asleep, and Lulu was keeping watch over both of them."

"I don't see what was so funny," said Rosemary distantly. "I suppose that makes me not only wholesome but idiotic."

"It makes you lucky. And me a creep with a perverted sense of humor. There isn't anything funny about wanting to kill somebody you love. There isn't anything reasonable about it, either. All the same, it happens. But you don't believe that, do you, Rosemary? You're one of the lucky ones that never get love and hate mixed up. Or maybe you've never been in love."

"I guess I haven't," said Rosemary. "At least not that way." She took a deep breath. "You have been? You mean it was like that with you and Joyce?"

"I mean—" he began roughly. But he bit it off there. For a moment he glared at her, then buried his face in his hands. His voice came out, muffled but savage. "Why don't you get out of here? Beat it. Go home."

"If you want me to." She waited, but he did not answer.

She looked back from the door. He was still hunched in the chair, face hidden, fingers knotted in his hair.

chapter 6

Martin held out for two days: on Wednesday he called Rosemary and asked—oh, very casually—if she would by any chance be interested in having a drink with him after work.

"Fine. Where?" she said.

He was so effectively braced for a refusal that this answer threw him all off balance. "What? Oh. Good. About six, then?"

"Where?" she repeated, and he named The Peacock because it was a fixture in the neighborhood of his apartment and the first place that came to mind. As soon as he hung up, of course, he thought of any number of spots that would have been more glamorous or exciting. But if he called her back he might seem to be making too much of a production out of what was supposed to be an ordinary, spur-of-the-moment invitation. Better to let well enough alone.

He got there at five thirty, early enough to snag one of

the tables outdoors; during the summer The Peacock went Continental with a sidewalk cafe. It was gritty but cheerful sitting there in the slanting sunshine behind the boxed shrubs that separated customers from passers-by. Yes, very cheerful to be waiting for Rosemary, who was still willing to see him again, in spite of his disgraceful behavior the other night. The waiting might be more pleasant than the actual seeing, he thought with his habitual pessimism: face to face with her, he might be too overcome with the shameful memory of their last meeting to enjoy the present one. For he had come within a hair's breadth of spilling the whole miserable business to her, had drawn back just in time. And then to pack her off like that, as if she were to blame. . .

The fact remained that she had agreed to come tonight. For whatever reason, time would tell. At the moment he refused to pick holes in the bright surface of the fact that remained. He sipped his gin and tonic and turned a benign eye on his fellow customers. Two of them were obviously also waiting for someone: the fellow with the profile and the drawing pad at the next table, who pretended to be busy sketching the passing scene; and, at the other end, the girl who alternated between nervous glances at her watch and clinical inspections of her face in her compact mirror. Others—like the two young couples, complete with babies and dogs; the pair of pretty boys; and the elderly man with his beer and evening newspaper—were settled for an hour's relaxation, absorbed in their own conversations or thoughts. As Martin and Rosemary would soon be: she would be right here, in the chair opposite him, with her butterscotch-and-molasses hair tethered in a topknot, and her round tanned arms and her summery dress. . .

This agreeable reverie was interrupted. "Pardon me, can you tell me the time?" It was the fellow with the sketch pad, openly restive by now. He turned toward Martin. His face, so handsome in profile, was unexpectedly ordinary when seen head on. The droop to his mouth now seemed less sensitive than weak; his hairline was no longer distinguished, but simply receding; the whole effect subtly coarsened. His smile was engaging, though, and his voice had vibrancy and depth. Almost an actor's voice, Martin thought. There was nothing theatrical—or artistic, either, when it came to that—about his clothes: gray summer suit, modest figured tie.

He gave a helpless little shrug when Martin told him it was a quarter of six. "Oh well, she's only half an hour late. No cause for alarm. There must be some punctual women in the world, but I don't know them. Do you?"

"I hope so," said Martin. The possibility of Rosemary's being late, which had not occurred to him before, instantly burgeoned into a near-certainty. With ramifications: she might not come at all. Probably wouldn't. Probably had seen his call as a heaven-sent opportunity to pay him back. "How long is cause for alarm? An hour?"

"Depends. I'm an easygoing type, myself. I always give them the benefit of the doubt. Could be I misunderstood the time, or even the place."

"There's only one Peacock. As far as I know."

"I was just generalizing. She picked the spot. I've never been here before. Nice, isn't it? I'm getting quite attached to it. And then I came prepared." He patted his sketch pad. "Something told me it was going to be like this. It's an ego-building device. Gives her a sense of power to keep me waiting."

Yes indeed. Martin decided to change the subject. "You're a professional artist?"

"Not with a capital A. Commercial stuff. Free lance. But I keep dabbling, just to prove I was meant for finer things. It's my ego-building device, I suppose. We all have them." He turned on the engaging smile. "Right?"

Maybe that was Martin's trouble. No ego-building device. Unless you wanted to count Rosemary, who could just as easily turn out to be very much the contrary. "Well," he began. But at that moment his fellow-philosopher sprang up, hand out-stretched. He at least had not waited in vain.

During their conversation Martin had been sitting with his back to the entrance; now he turned, mildly curious about what sort of girl it would be. The mental image he had built up—for no particular reason—was of a model-type, all bones and high style.

So it was with a double start of astonishment that he saw Thelma Holm threading her way between the rows of tables. She looked better put together than usual: the full skirt she was wearing was becoming to her slim figure, her bangs were brushed, the rest of her straight brown hair was pinned up smoothly, in a way that showed off her well-shaped head. But she was still a long way from high style.

She did not see Martin until he stumbled to his feet and gulped out a surprised "Hello." Then she stopped in her tracks, and her face flooded with color, the slow, painful flush of an embarrassment so acute that it communicated itself to him. If the table had been big enough, he would gladly have crawled under it. And if she had spotted him in time, she would have turned tail and fled. He was sure of it.

"You know each other?" asked the fellow with the profile. He sounded pleased and amused, not in the least embarrassed. Well, why should he be? Why should anybody be?

"Of course. Martin, how nice to see you!" After the first bad moment Thelma pulled herself together. A little too much chattering and exclaiming, maybe, but it was that kind of situation. What a coincidence. What a small world. She performed the introductions. Martin Shipley. Bob—White. Like that, with a definite pause in the middle, and a stress on the White, as if she had pounced on it. Or—more likely, thought Martin, observing Mr. White's slightly lifted eyebrow—plucked it out of thin air.

Martin hurried to explain that he was waiting for Rosemary. In other words, trapped; he did not want Thelma to think he was sticking around to spy on her, or to gloat over her discomfiture. Whatever its source, it was her business. By now she seemed to have talked most of it away. She was off that miserable wagon, hooray. Well, one foot off. Still in the experimental stage, but last night she had had one drink, only one, so she felt she could be trusted again tonight. Wasn't it wonderful?

She looked from one to the other of them, her face alight with hope and that other quality, the hyper-responsiveness that made her seem so vulnerable. (The word that had sprung into Martin's mind when he first met her. Here it was again.) Too susceptible to other people for her own good; she was bound to get hurt over and over again, in the future as she undoubtedly had been in the past. By Vic, Enid, perhaps in some mysterious way by this White fellow, possibly even by Martin himself. . .

He caught sight of Rosemary, and stopped worrying about Thelma or anything else. Not even ignominious memories could mar the moment of Rosemary's arrival on time. Pink dress, rose-fresh face, sunny hair. His head swam with jubilance. There was another spate of exclamations. Another set of introductions. Bob—White. (Again Thelma brought it out with that curious little pause-and-pounce effect.) Mr. White's inspection of Rosemary was thorough and appreciative. Also a bit surprised: he too must have built up a mental image of Martin's girl, and it didn't match with the reality any more than the model-type Martin had dreamed up for him. So he had expected a droop, had he? Ha!

Once more Thelma went into a fit of nervous talking. "Bob's going to do us some murals," she explained, a little feverishly. "At least I hope so. I'm counting on you, Bob, to come up with some ideas about what to do with those living room walls. If not murals then something else. They paralyze me. I mean it. When I look at them I lapse into a kind of coma." She took a swig of her one drink and glanced at her watch. "I don't want to hurry you, Bob, but I really would like to have you view the remains and see what you think. . ."

"Whenever you say. You're the boss," said Bob White with cheerful deference. He had been uncommonly quiet since Thelma showed up. Letting her run the show. Possibly waiting for her to feed him his lines. Now he added one of his own. "You and Vic, I should say."

"Oh, but I want to surprise Vic! I mean, he's not to know until it's all worked out. You mustn't breathe a word to Vic, any of you, about any of this." She made flustered, anxious gestures with her hands. The flush was back in her face. "You won't, will you?"

"Of course not," Martin assured her.

"Lucky I mentioned it," said Bob easily. "I might have let the cat out of the bag."

They left very shortly, Thelma with her head high, Bob carefully not taking her arm until they reached the corner.

There was a busy silence. Then Rosemary said, "Murals, my eye."

Martin had been thinking very much the same thing. But for some reason he resented hearing it put into words. "I don't know what you mean by that," he said stiffly.

"Oh come on, Martin. It was perfectly obvious what's going on. She made up the murals on the spur of the moment, just like she did his name. The Bob part may be okay, probably is, but I'll bet anything you like his last name isn't White."

"That may prove something to you. It doesn't to me. And I fail to see anything out of the way about Thelma's having a sociable drink with the guy, whatever his name happens to be. What the hell of it?"

"Nothing. My point exactly. I wouldn't have given it a second thought, nobody would have, if she hadn't gone into such a swivet. Don't tell me you didn't notice how jumpy she was. Guilty conscience. It was written all over her."

"What about him? He didn't act to me like a man weighted down with sinful secrets."

"I expect he's an old hand at the game," said Rosemary. "Actually, he's very good-looking from the side."

"Sure. He'd be great stamped on a coin."

"My, you're grumpy. I shouldn't think you'd begrudge

Thelma a little fling of her own. Personally, I think it serves Vic right."

"So do I. If that's what she's doing." After a pause, he added reluctantly, "And I suppose she is. This White guy really is an artist, though. He was sitting here sketching while he waited for her. Look, he forgot his sketch pad."

It was still lying on one of the chairs at the adjoining table. Martin picked it up and flipped through the pages. Pretty undistinguished stuff. Well, Bob White had not pretended otherwise. His ego-building device.

"But if it was just a matter of murals," Rosemary began.

"I know. Why would she meet him here, instead of just having him come up to the apartment? And then that business about not telling Vic. That sounded fishy, I admit. In fact—" He looked across at her and lost the thread, simply let it sweep away in another flood of jubilance at the miracle of Rosemary's being here.

"I was so afraid you wouldn't come tonight," he said in a rush.

"Why on earth wouldn't I? I said I would."

"I know. But I thought maybe you— On account of the other night. You must have thought I'd gone crazy. Maybe you still do."

"No, or I wouldn't be here," said Rosemary. Her clear hazel eyes met his unflinchingly. "It was my fault for mentioning Joyce. But it seemed to me maybe you wanted to talk about her, and I thought if you did—"

"If I did you'd listen and pat my hand and feel sorry for me. Oh God, here I go again. Saying things I don't want to. Not saying things I. . . That's always my trouble. I'm not sure myself, I mean, about myself. Not sure about anything. I probably am crazy."

"Means nothing," said Rosemary briskly. "I'm not always sure about myself, either. And I'm so wholesome it's disgusting."

"I never said disgusting." He put his hand over hers; it was square and forthright, the kind of competent little paw Rosemary would have. So different from Joyce's hand—tapering, beautiful, useless—that it might have belonged to another species. Was that what drew him to Rosemary, the contrast between her and all that he had once loved and hated and agonized over? Or was it the contrast between his own nature with its endless convolutions and self-examinations, and Rosemary's straightforward approach to life? It was typical of him to be wasting this very moment, which ought to be pure enjoyment, in futile speculation. Futile and ludicrous: the really unfathomable mystery was what drew Rosemary to him. "And now I wonder if you're all that wholesome."

"Why?"

"Because you're here," he said. "That's what beats me. You're here with me instead of—"

"Hi, kids. Still here, I see." It was Bob White back again, alone this time, looking for his sketch pad. Think of the loss to posterity, if it had been swept out with the empty bottles! No no, he mustn't stay, he didn't want to muscle in. . . Well, if they were sure, and only if he could buy them a drink. . .

He sat down, beaming, especially at Rosemary, who said brightly, "Did you get the murals settled already?"

"Good Lord, I'm not that fast a worker! No, as it turned out, Vic got home early, so the murals will have to wait. Thelma and her surprises. Chances are she'll forget and let it out, if she hasn't already. She doesn't have the temperament for secrets."

"I shouldn't think so, from what I've seen of her," said Martin. "I take it you're an old friend of hers?"

"Well, not a close friend. I knew her and Vic slightly when they were living in Philadelphia. I put in a stretch there myself, several years ago. A brief stretch, mercifully. Hadn't seen either of them since, until just recently. Cheers. To the murals. I don't mind admitting, I jumped at the chance. Free lancing can be pretty poor pickings at times. But it still beats the old nine-to-five weekly pay check rat race. For my money. I don't know how you guys in the architecture racket feel about it, but—"

"Architecture? I'm with a publishing company. Where'd you get that idea?"

"Snatched it out of the air, I guess. Thelma said something about having met you through Vic, so I took it from there. No hard feelings, I hope."

"Of course no hard feelings. I only wish it were so. Actually, the way I met Vic—" He hesitated over Enid's name. But Bob White must already know, involved as he pretty obviously was with Thelma. Who didn't have the temperament for secrets. "Well. It was through Enid Baxter," he said, and instantly regretted it.

But why? Nothing happened, nothing in the least sensational. Very carefully, Bob White set his glass down. "Oh? You knew Enid Baxter?"

"Yes. Quite well. Rosemary knew her too. She and Rosemary's mother were in business together. Didn't Thelma tell you?"

"No. No, she didn't. I didn't realize. . ." He could hardly say anything else, of course, not and maintain the gentlemanly pretense that he and Thelma were only casual acquaintances. "A terrible thing. Terrible. Not that I really knew Enid Baxter. Just to speak to, back there in Philadelphia. But her name rang a bell, when I saw it in the papers, and then of course the picture of her. She had the kind of face you don't forget. It shook me up, but good. I can imagine what it must have done to her friends. . . They haven't found the guy that did it, have they? I suppose it was one of these crazy kids. Or maybe a junkie."

"Maybe," said Martin. "They haven't come up with any other answer. Or if they have they're keeping it quiet."

"They sure are. They must have gone through her private life with a fine-toothed comb, but there wasn't the slightest hint in the papers of anything suspicious. I should think, if there had been, the reporter lads would have gotten wind of it. They're a pack of bloodhounds. It's a wonder to me they didn't rake up all the old dirt— Sorry. I shouldn't have said that."

"If you mean about Enid and Vic," said Rosemary, "it's all right. We already know. So do the police. They questioned everybody in her address book, and the Holms were there, because she'd run into them recently here in New York. So of course it all came out."

"Yes. Bound to. Well, it never was much of a secret. The gossips had a field day. But then it all blew over. Enid came to New York, and that was the end of it." His smile, which could be so engaging, now seemed to Martin vaguely unpleasant. It was like the difference between his profile and full face: something about him that kept Martin swinging between like and dislike. "And a lucky thing for Vic. It could have been—well, let's say a little awkward, if he'd been mixed up with her at this stage of the game. He'd have had to come up with one hell of an alibi."

"Oh, we all had alibis," Rosemary assured him blithely. "Martin was on vacation, and Mother was at the movies, and I was in Connecticut, and the Holms had a week end guest from Philadelphia. The three of them spent a quiet evening at home. So it couldn't have been anybody who knew her. That leaves a prowler, and if they ever catch him it will just be a fluke, I suppose. She wasn't robbed, so there's nothing to trace." Nothing except the jade ring, Martin thought; it must have slipped Rosemary's mind, or she'd spill that along with everything else she knew. He concentrated, willing her to get to work on her drink. At this rate they'd be stuck with Bob White for the rest of the evening. But—the perils of thought transference—she missed that message and picked up the other one. "Well, there was one thing missing, her jade ring. But that doesn't necessarily mean it was stolen. She could easily have lost it, it was too big for her."

"Funny she wasn't robbed, if it was a prowler." It was a perfunctory comment; Bob White's interest was obviously waning.

"Something scared him off," Rosemary explained. "Either that, or he just panicked and ran when he realized he'd killed her."

"Yes. Probably. . . Hey, it must be late, time I shoved off and left you to your own devices." He finished his drink and drew out his wallet. "No, no," he went on, as Martin started to protest, "this is on me. You can buy me a drink some time when I'm broke. I often am. No kidding, I've enjoyed this. Let's get together again—that is, if you'd like to."

Once more—partly because he was leaving?—Martin liked him, envied him his easy sociability and his poise under circumstances that might have been embarrassing, had been acutely so, to Thelma. He scribbled Martin's office phone number in his sketch pad (but not Rosemary's: another point to his credit); he himself was in the process of moving, so it would be simpler for him to call Martin. Which he might never do at all. Still, it was a nice gesture.

He shook hands with them both and was off, a brisk, average-looking fellow, neither young nor old, rich nor poor, handsome nor ugly. They watched till he reached the corner and, with a last wave in their direction, disappeared.

Then Rosemary sighed. "I wish I hadn't talked so much," she said.

chapter 7

"Mrs. Nicholson?"

He had a pleasant voice, and an air of tentative friendliness. He hesitated just inside the office door, not barging in the way some salesmen did. That was what Hazel took him for: a salesman of some kind. Furniture or rugs, probably. He had a brief case under his arm; he was well dressed, in other words unobtrusively; and his profile reminded her fleetingly, very fleetingly, of John Barrymore.

"It's all right," she said when he apologized for interrupting her work. More than all right; she was so frustrated by the problem living room she had been grappling with that any distraction would have been welcome. She pushed the plans to one side and gestured toward the chair opposite her desk. "Come on in. What's on your mind?"

"I'm Bob White, Mrs. Nicholson." He gave her a sincere handshake and sat down, smiling. "I met your daughter last night. Rosemary."

"Oh?" For some reason it gave her an odd little turn. Rosemary's friends often dropped in, and they were more often than not strangers to Hazel. College kids. Not that this fellow was old, exactly, but he was no college kid. No salesman either, apparently. "Rosemary's not here. I don't know whether she'll be back this afternoon or not."

"That's what I get for not calling first. Actually, it was all unpremeditated. I just thought I'd take a chance and pop in, as long as I happened to be in the neighborhood anyway."

"I see," said Hazel. Now that she was facing him, she decided she didn't care much for his looks. Definitely too old for Rosemary; not her type at all. "Well. I'll tell her you were here."

"What I wanted to ask her— You wouldn't by any chance know, would you? Where I can get hold of Martin Shipley?"

"You know Martin Shipley?" This also surprised her, and not just because he didn't seem like Martin's type, either. Rosemary hadn't mentioned meeting any friends or acquaintances of Martin's. Hadn't mentioned Martin himself, in fact, except to say that he had checked with the police about Enid's jade ring so Hazel needn't bother. It was Hazel's impression that this bit of information had been relayed via the telephone. No reason to get upset or hurt, of course, simply because Rosemary ("Please, Mom, I'm not a three-year-old child!") had neglected to give a complete, detailed account of how and with whom she had spent every single minute of the last few days.

"I met him and Rosemary last night," Bob White was saying, and then he launched into a complicated story that she didn't follow too closely. The name of Thelma Holm, which kept cropping up, didn't immediately register with Hazel; she paid more attention after it did. "I wrote Martin's office number down somewhere," he finished, "and now I can't find it. Don't even know what publishing company he's with. But I did remember Rosemary's saying you were Enid Baxter's partner—I knew her, you know, not well, but still—and as I say, I was in the neighborhood, so I thought I'd give it a try. I'd like to call Martin for lunch. Awfully nice guy."

Hazel had thought so, too; still did, in spite of that business about his wife. Which was another thing Rosemary hadn't mentioned since Saturday afternoon, when she had blurted it out, with such painful results. Not a word, though she knew how much it had disturbed Hazel. "I don't have his office number," she said, "but I can give you his number at home. He lives in the same house Enid did, you know."

"Really? I didn't realize that. Good Lord, then, he must have been right in the middle of the whole thing!"

"If you mean the night it happened, he wasn't. He was out of town. But he was a good friend of Enid's, probably as close a friend as she had." She caught the expression on his face, and added curtly, "I don't mean boy friend."

"No, of course not. Aside from the difference in their ages, Martin's just not. . . Well, she was quite a dream boat. Or so I gather."

"I thought you said you knew her."

"Only slightly. And it was several years ago, in Philadelphia. The Holms were living there then too." He paused, in case Hazel cared to comment. She did not. "I didn't realize they'd gotten together again here in New York. Enid and Vic Holm."

Hazel eyed him with cold distaste. There were several

answers she could give him. *What makes you think they had?* Or, *I have no idea what you're referring to.* Or, *What of it?* But any of these could be twisted around into the confirmation he was fishing for. So could the silence she was preserving, she realized with a sinking sensation.

At least she had the satisfaction of staring him down. He was bright enough to know he had made a tactical error. And cowardly enough to turn tail. Fumbling with his brief case, smiling abjectly, spilling over with thanks and other inanities, he scuttled out the door.

All right, he had gotten Martin's address and telephone number out of her. Big deal. If not out of her, then out of the phone book. That had been only an excuse, anyway. What he was really after. . . Rosemary? Possibly. Probably. In any case, Hazel decided, it was time for a word or two with that young lady.

She turned up shortly afterwards, and—as might have been expected—took a highhanded attitude about the whole thing. "Honestly, Mother. I don't know what you were thinking of, handing out Martin's phone number like that."

"It's a state secret? Anyway, look who's talking about handing out information. You must have given out with a few vital statistics yourself." Rosemary's face turned red, and Hazel pushed on. "To him, not to me. I didn't even know you'd been seeing Martin."

"Didn't I tell you he called me? How could it have slipped my mind, an earth-shaking news item like that? You'd think he was Richard Burton or something."

"Don't be fresh," said Hazel absent-mindedly. "After what happened Saturday afternoon, I didn't think either of us would ever hear from him again."

"Oh well, all that nonsense." Rosemary fluffed her hair. "Matter of fact, Mom, I'm supposed to bring you down to his place for a drink tonight."

"Me? You're supposed to—"

"He likes you. I can't imagine why. You'll come, won't you? You're not doing anything else?"

"Not a thing," Hazel assured her. "I'll be delighted."

"Good. You can apologize for talking out of turn to Bob Whoever-he-is."

"All right, but I still don't—"

"And listen, Mom, you won't say anything about the Joyce business, will you? I mean, no use hashing over things like that. He broods too much, as it is. Forget I ever told you."

"I'll try not to disgrace you," said Hazel drily.

It was impossible, of course, to forget the Joyce business. All the more so with Rosemary in this much of a flap over Martin Shipley. But previous flaps had taught Hazel the weaknesses—indeed, the dangers—of maternal opposition. The folk singer, for instance, had stayed in the picture an extra month solely because she had not kept her mouth shut about him. She mustn't make that mistake with Martin. Wait and see. Play it cool. If push came to shove, then would be time enough to hash over the Joyce business, once and for all.

It could be worse, she told herself glumly on the way down to Martin's apartment. It could be Bob White or whatever his name was, instead of Martin. Besides, there was Enid's endorsement of Martin, the obviously genuine friendship between them. . .

Yes, and look at what had happened to Enid.

With a profound sigh, she heaved herself out of the cab, tucked in her blouse, and trudged after Rosemary.

Who had bounced up to the door and was already ringing Martin's bell.

He looked quite spruce in his seersucker jacket, obviously primed for inspection by the older generation. Rosemary must have given him an advance briefing, too, thought Hazel; no wonder he seemed so nervous.

But that was only part of it. It turned out that he had another worry: a third guest, unexpected and uninvited, who had appeared ten minutes ago and whose dominating presence seemed to fill Martin's living room and imbue his little party with a color altogether different from that originally planned.

Vic Holm, master of all he surveyed, stood beside his chair waiting to be introduced. He was a big man (as Hazel preferred men to be), big and fair-haired and blunt-featured. He was not handsome, as Enid had been beautiful; but never mind non-essentials. Hazel, remembering those other shadowy "beaus," had no trouble recognizing that in him Enid had met her match.

"Oh yes, Enid's partner," he said as he shook her hand. His gray eyes met hers without self-consciousness; all the same, there was something disquieting about them. She thought of desert, wilderness, desolation.

Then he turned to Rosemary, smiling down at her, openly enjoying her fresh prettiness. And don't think she wasn't smiling back. Well, who wouldn't? "I've heard a lot about you too, Rosemary. Nice to meet you. . . Want me to tend bar, Martin? I'll be glad to."

But Martin was determined to hang on to at least this vestige of control over the proceedings. He set up a remarkable clatter with the ice and glasses, and when he served the drinks narrowly missed spilling Rosemary's in her lap. Nerves, no doubt. Or could it be repressed hostility toward Vic?

If so, it did not bother Vic. He downed his drink—a straight shot—at one gulp and plunged without delay into what did bother him. "You don't happen to know where Thelma is, do you, Rosemary?"

"Thelma? She's missing?"

"Lost, stolen, strayed. Last seen drinking." He caught Hazel's eye and smiled grimly. "My wife, Mrs. Nicholson. In case you're interested."

"But she was all right when we saw her last night. Wasn't she, Martin? She only had one drink."

"She went on from there. When I saw her last night, believe me, she was far from all right. I don't know where she went after she left The Peacock, but she must have taken the long way home. I didn't get in myself until after midnight, and I'd been there at least an hour before she came rolling in."

"After midnight? But I thought—" A look flashed from Martin to Rosemary, and she hastily shifted gears. "I mean, when did she disappear?"

"How the hell do I know? I gave up and went to bed about three, and when I woke up this morning she was gone. I've been calling everybody I can think of all day, and. . ." He pressed his hands against his temples in a sudden, brief gesture of weary despair. "I don't know what to do," he said quietly.

There was a moment of tense silence. "How about Philadelphia?" Martin asked. "That friend of yours, Lulu McGrath?"

"I thought of her first, of course. She and her husband are off on a cruise. Won't be back till next week. I wish to

God Lulu *was* around. She's better at coping with these crises than I am."

"It's happened before?"

"In Philadelphia. Not here. If she doesn't show up pretty soon, I'll have to call the police. Or maybe I shouldn't wait, maybe I ought to—"

"Wait!" Martin cleared his throat and went on more calmly. "It's a little soon for that, isn't it? I'd give her another couple of hours. Did she seem upset about anything last night?"

"I suppose you mean did we have a fight," said Vic. "Thelma's always upset when she goes on a binge. Not about anything in particular. Just life in general. To tell you the truth, I don't pay much attention when she gets to maundering on. She seemed on the verge of passing out, so I figured it was safe for me to go to bed. My mistake. I remembered she mentioned your name a couple of times, that's why I came over here."

It didn't really answer the question of whether or not they had quarreled, thought Hazel. But she didn't like to press the point. Certainly there was nothing in Vic's manner to suggest evasion. He couldn't have sounded more candid. Or more tired. That was what impressed her most, and of course it made sense. No matter how devoted you might be to a drunk, in the end you just got tired. She wished she could think of something helpful. "You've checked with Bob Whats-his-name, I suppose," she said. "Bob White."

This harmless remark had a startling effect—at least on Rosemary and Martin. She caught her breath audibly; he stiffened. Both of them darted nervous glances at Vic, who merely looked blank and asked, "Bob who? Bob White? Who's he?"

Hazel, aware that she had somehow or other put her foot in her mouth, sent forth a silent plea for help. But neither of them even looked at her. There was nothing to do but blunder on. "Well, I understood, that is, I thought Rosemary said. . ."

"Rosemary said what?" Vic's voice crackled with impatience. "What is all this, anyway? I don't know any Bob White."

Rosemary remained dumb. After a couple of false starts Martin got it out. "He was there last night too. At The Peacock. With Thelma."

"You mean she wasn't by herself? Why didn't you say so in the first place? Who is this guy? Let's get hold of him and—"

"I haven't any idea where he lives. Probably in a hotel. I'm not even sure about his name. He seemed to know you and Thelma both, at least that's the impression I got."

"You're a big help," said Vic bitterly. "You were there too, Rosemary. What impression did you get, if any?"

"The same as Martin's," Rosemary snapped back. But then she smiled—a little too disarmingly, in Hazel's opinion—and switched to a tone of frank confession. "Oh well, it can't make that much difference now. Can it, Martin? Even though we promised. Bob's supposed to do some murals for your living room, only Thelma wanted to surprise you, you see. That's why we didn't mention him before."

"Murals? He's an artist?"

"Mostly commercial stuff. Free lance. I think he said he used to live in Philadelphia."

There was a silence. Under Vic's unnerving scrutiny Rosemary managed to hang on to her guileless expression. Martin, whose turn came next, shuffled his feet unhappily. "It still doesn't ring any bells with me," Vic said at last. "I wonder how many Bob Whites there are in the phone book."

A column and a half, it turned out, none of whom had chosen to identify himself as a commercial artist. And Martin pointed out, for the second time, that they were not even sure about the name. It was certainly the name he had given Hazel, but she refrained from calling any further attention to herself by saying so. After all, she too had sensed something fishy about the fellow.

"Maybe he's the mysterious phone caller I had after I got home from the office this afternoon," Vic was going on. "It happened twice. When I answered, nobody said anything. Just hung up without saying a word. If they were cooking up this mural surprise, I suppose it could have been him, trying to get Thelma. But in that case he can't know where she is either. I mean, if he expected her to be home— Oh God. I don't know. I just thought, if they did go on a pub-crawl together last night after they left The Peacock—"

"He came back by himself," Rosemary said. "Half an hour or so later, to get his sketch pad. He forgot and left it the first time. We were still there, and he had another drink with us."

"He could have met her again later, though," Vic persisted. "If he did, she might have hit some of the same spots when she went out by herself the second time around. It would at least give me something to go on." He sighed and stood up. "I've taken up enough of your time. I'll go home and start calling up Bob Whites. By the way, what did he look like?"

"Just an average sort of guy," Martin said. "I'd say

about thirty-five. Medium brown hair and eyes. He was better looking from the side than head on."

Vic paused at the door, absorbing these meager clues. He did not comment on them. "Okay. If you hear anything, you'll let me know, won't you? Sorry to bother you with my problems."

As soon as he was gone Rosemary burst out like a faucet turned on full force. "Do you think he bought it, about the murals? I didn't see anything to do but tell him, once Mom let it out. Not that I'm blaming you, Mom, how were you to know? If I'd had any idea he was going to be here. . . And you just sat there like a bump on a log, Martin. Somebody had to say something. Besides, I felt so sorry for him."

"Oh sure," said Martin. "A very pathetic fellow. My heart bleeds for him."

"I don't know what you mean by that! Anybody could see how upset he was about Thelma. Absolutely distraught."

"He was upset, all right. The question is, why? You'll notice he didn't commit himself on whether or not they had a fight last night. For all we know, he could have beaten Thelma up and now he's worried because she walked out on him and he doesn't know what she might do next. It's just his word she was drunk, and somebody's lying, that's for sure. Vic says he didn't get home till after midnight, but according to Bob White he was already there when he took Thelma home from The Peacock."

"Oh well, Bob White! If you're going to believe what he said!"

"Listen, you two." Hazel took a deep breath. "Would you mind telling me what this is all about?"

"Don't be obtuse, Mom. We were keeping quiet about

Bob White because we think Thelma's got something going with him. You know? An extra-marital affair. I don't believe that's his real name, any more than I believe the phoney murals business. She's probably shacked up with him right now."

"Oh," said Hazel feebly. "Well. I never thought of that. I mean, she must be out of her mind. A husband like Vic, and she takes up with—" She remembered Enid, and realized she was being obtuse again. Was that why Martin was taking such an anti-Vic stand, because he resented the fact that Enid had once been in love with Vic? Had once been. Might well have been right up to the day she died. "That Bob White," Hazel said slowly, "or whatever his name is. Did you get the feeling there was something off-color about him? I don't mean because of Thelma. I didn't even know about that angle when I saw him."

"You saw him?" Martin asked in astonishment. "When was that? I thought you'd just heard about him from Rosemary."

"He came into the shop this afternoon. Claimed he'd lost your telephone number and wanted to get it from Rosemary. I apologize for giving it to him, by the way. He remembered I was in business with Enid, you see. I guess that's what put me off about him. He was so almighty interested in Enid."

After a moment Martin said, "Some people are like that. Morbid curiosity. No need for you to apologize. I gave him my phone number myself, last night. Now then. How about another drink? And then maybe a bite of dinner somewhere?"

"Not me, thank you," said Hazel, who had been strictly and thoroughly trained in the deportment proper for a parent. She was rewarded with a positive gust of grateful relief from both sides. "I've got to figure out that so-and-so living room some time between now and tomorrow morning. Don't be too late, Rosemary. Awfully nice to see you again, Martin."

She meant it. He was as nice a lad, Martin Shipley, as anybody could ask for. It occurred to her, on the way home in the cab he put her into—with alacrity, but also with a shy and surprising little kiss on her cheek—that she had not thought once about the Joyce business during the course of his little party. She wondered if she would have, without the distraction of Vic Holm.

chapter 8

When he came back from seeing Rosemary home, she was there waiting for him. Thelma. Sitting on the concrete slab that edged his four square feet of garden, so quiet and motionless that he all but stumbled over her.

"Martin?" she whispered. "It is you, isn't it? I thought you'd never come."

"Thelma! Are you all right? Vic was here earlier, looking for you. Nobody knew where you were."

"I don't know either," she said, and laughed dimly. "Can I come inside with you, Martin? Please? Just for a while. I don't know anybody else. I don't know many people here in New York."

She did not seem particularly drunk to him. No lurching on her way inside; no marked slurring in her speech. While he unlocked the door to his apartment, she stood close to him, peering fearfully up the shadowy flight of stairs. "She lived up there, didn't she? Somebody ran down the stairs. I read in the paper. The neighbor woman heard somebody running down the stairs."

"Come on in, Thelma." He flipped on the light and steered her inside. "Sit down. Would you like some coffee?"

"All right," she said docilely. "Thank you."

Last night she had looked unusually neat and crisp in her full skirt with the belt that cinched in her slim waist. Tonight her dress was rumpled and soiled; her hair straggled about her face, which looked drawn and shiny, devoid of make-up. She huddled in the corner of the couch, easing her feet out of her high-heeled pumps. He sat down beside her while the coffee perked.

"Have you talked to Vic? Does he know you're here?" She shook her head no. "I think we ought to call him, then. He was worried about you. So was I."

"Did he tell you I was drunk? He did, didn't he?" She seemed oddly pleased, almost as if she were proud of herself. "Shame on me," she said, and wriggled her toes.

Food, he thought; she's probably famished. But she only nibbled at the crackers and cheese he brought in with the coffee. "You're awfully good to me," she said. "I was afraid you'd be mad. But I couldn't think of anywhere else to go."

"You could go home, you know. Couldn't you?" She did not answer. Her eyes shifted away from his to a point in the middle of the rug. She sat still, knotted up with tension. "Why not? Are you afraid of Vic?"

"Of course not," she said quickly. "Why should I be afraid of Vic?"

"I don't know. I thought you might have had some kind of a quarrel last night. About your drinking, maybe. Or. . . Listen, Thelma, he knows you saw Bob White last night. I'm sorry. I didn't mean to tell him, but Rosemary and her mother were here and—well, it came out."

"Oh," she whispered. She did look at him now, out of big, unfathomable eyes. "Did he— What did he say?"

"Naturally he was anxious to get hold of the guy. But nobody knew how or where to reach him. The name didn't seem to mean anything to Vic. That was it, wasn't it? Bob White?"

"Yes. Bob—White." Again she wriggled her toes.

"It doesn't matter, I guess, now that you're back. If you won't call Vic, Thelma, I'm going to. Somebody has to. Otherwise he's going to report you missing to the police."

"No! Oh no!"

"Yes. Oh yes. He was threatening to do it while he was here." Seriously or not? Martin was still wondering about that, among other things—including what was actually at the root of Vic's concern and worry. But it wasn't safe to pooh-pooh either the threats or the concern: whatever had gone on between the Holms last night, Thelma's whereabouts could not be kept a secret from Vic. If she expected Martin to connive at any such goings-on she had come to the wrong place. "I talked him into waiting a bit."

"I see," she said gravely. "That was nice of you. It would have been awfully embarrassing, wouldn't it, to be plucked out of the gutter by the police. If that's where I was."

So that was to be her line: complete lapse of memory. Well, it was probably as good as any, as far as Vic was concerned. Martin himself was suddenly tired of the whole slippery conversation. Whatever she had turned to him for—sanctuary, moral support, a breathing space before she faced Vic—he was willing to supply, up to a point. But they could at least be honest with each other.

"Oh, come on, Thelma," he said. "You know perfectly

well where you were. At least part of the time. So do I. Don't worry, I'm not going to give you and Bob White away. Or whatever his name is. You can save your blank mind business, and the phoney murals, and all the rest of it, for Vic. Please. Don't waste it on me."

"What do you mean? What are you talking about?" She turned on him, shivering with anger, outrage, fear—he did not know what. "Do you think Bob White and I. . ." Her voice trailed off; her mouth remained a little open, and trembling.

"Of course I think Bob White and you," said Martin wearily. "It was written all over you when you walked into The Peacock last night and saw me. You looked guilty as hell. Ready to sink through the floor. Why would you act like that if you were just having an innocent drink with a casual acquaintance? You wouldn't. It simply doesn't make sense. I don't know how long you've been carrying on your little hush-hush romance, and I don't care, but you obviously need more practice when it comes to managing it."

"Oh dear," she said, in a stricken voice. And again her mood switched; a fit of giggles seized her, uncontrollable as hiccups. "Oh dear, and I thought I was being so clever . . . I'm sorry, Martin, I just. . . Yes, of course. Doesn't make sense. . ." She leaned back, gulping and swiping at the tears that ran down her face. Watching her, Martin had to laugh too, though her lack of restraint made him a little uncomfortable. Drunks always affected him that way, and he realized now that she must be much less sober than he had thought at first. Eventually she pulled herself together and asked, with a fresh flicker of alarm, "Does Vic know? Is that why he was so anxious to get hold of Bob, because he thought we were together?"

"How do I know what Vic thinks? About anything? I certainly didn't tell him, but he may have guessed. You could have let it out yourself, when you saw him last night. Can't you remember anything you said to each other before he went to bed and you sailed out again?"

She shook her head helplessly. "I expect he was mad at me. Or not mad exactly. Exasperated. Disgusted. You can't blame him. And I usually get on a crying jag. Because I'm so ashamed. . . I remember bits and pieces before I went home. I remember about Bob going back to The Peacock after his sketch pad. I waited for him at this other place, this place with the pink piano. It was a mistake to leave me alone, I kept having drinks while I waited for him."

"So that's how it was," said Martin. "Rosemary and I were still at The Peacock when he came back, you know. He sat down and had another drink with us. His story was that he had taken you home, only Vic was already there, so naturally nothing could be done about the murals. But then Vic said he didn't get home till after midnight, and it was even later when you hove in. So I couldn't help wondering—"

"Wondering who was lying, you mean?" She gave a dreary laugh. "Vic's got nothing to hide. Nothing to lie about any more. Not that he ever bothered to lie much, anyway. Everybody in Philadelphia knew about him and Enid, and he didn't care. Neither did she. They were past caring."

He hadn't left Thelma, though, thought Martin. How many times had he heard Enid say it? *Thelma won. He didn't leave her.* But would have this time—according to him—if death had not intervened. Not according to Enid, or Thelma either. Again, somebody was lying, and there was little doubt in Martin's mind as to who. The chances were that what Vic had to hide now would make the Philadelphia episode seem like innocent child's play.

"So why should I care if he knows about me and Bob?" Thelma was demanding belligerently. "Why should I lie to him about it? He'll find it out sooner or later anyway, the way he always finds out everything about me." Her eyes shifted to the telephone, and she shivered again. "If he doesn't like it, let him lump it. That's what I say. Isn't that right, Martin? Don't you think I ought to just tell him straight out?"

"Don't ask me, Thelma. You've got to tell him something, that's all I know about it. You can't put it off any longer."

"No. I can't, can I?" She stared at the telephone. Her hands remained locked in her lap. "I'll have to go home, won't I? I've got nowhere else to go."

"You could go to a hotel. I mean, if you're really that scared of Vic—"

"I'm not. Of course I'm not." Suddenly her hands unlocked; with a gesture of despair she snatched up the phone and dialled. Martin retreated to the kitchenette and clattered the coffee cups, to give her at least a semblance of privacy. He could still hear the murmur of her voice, and the click when she hung up. It was a very brief conversation.

"He's coming over to get me," she told Martin hopelessly. "Is that all right with you?"

"Yes, of course." Now that it was done—what he had urged her to do—he felt a surge of panic-stricken remorse. Who knew what Vic might do to her, once he got his hands on her? He was a violent man. A jealous man. And yet she would not admit that she was afraid of him.

Wifely loyalty. Love. Yes, she must love him very much, in spite of all she had suffered on his account.

She sat there so quietly, as if resigned to her doom. For an instant her eyes met Martin's, and it flashed through his mind like a streak of lightning—the possibility that she too knew, or at least suspected, the truth about Enid's death. Suspected was more likely, because she had been drunk that night, and probably had only a hazy impression to go on. But that would be enough for Vic (who always found out everything about her). No wonder her drinking worried him: loyal though she was, she might, in her cups, drop the one word or two that could destroy him. And no wonder she was frightened. . .

Only Lulu McGrath had been there too. There was no getting around Lulu. She had not been drunk. No hazy impressions for her; Vic could not have gone out that evening without her knowing it. And no wifely loyalty or love, either; she had no reason for reinforcing his alibi if she knew it was false. Could even Vic be persuasive or lucky enough to have not one but two women willing to cover up for him?

"If only Lulu were here," murmured Thelma, almost as if she had read Martin's mind. Then the doorbell rang, and she shrank back into the corner of the couch.

Vic's first words, when he strode in, were: "Thank God you called. Are you all right?" If there was an edge of irritation to his voice, there was certainly nothing that sounded like menace. And he bent over his errant wife rather tenderly, patting her hand. But then came the other questions. Where had she been? Why had she come here instead of home? Finally, of course: "Who's Bob White? This guy you met at The Peacock? Who is he?"

"You don't know him," Thelma said quickly. It was her

first coherent remark. She had burst into stagey, boozy tears at sight of Vic; had alternately clung to him and cowered away from him; had offered unintelligible sobs instead of answers. "He's just somebody I— Just because I was lonesome. Oh, I'm so ashamed! It's all over now, honestly, I promise you. I never want to see him again."

This information jolted Vic nicely. No doubt about it. His face stiffened. He blinked. "The murals? They said he was going to do some murals?"

"I had to tell them something. It was all I could think of. Silly of me. I shouldn't have tried to lie, it only made it worse." She gazed up at Vic pleadingly; it occurred to Martin that she might be hoping for an outburst of jealous rage, might be secretly enjoying the switch in circumstances that made her, for once, sinner instead of sinned against.

After a moment Vic said, "I see." He looked at Martin. "I gather you knew this all the time? You might have told me."

"Sure I might have. I don't happen to get my kicks out of running around tattling everything I know about other people's private affairs." And a damn lucky thing for you I don't, he added mentally. "I didn't ask to get in on any of this, and I'm sure as hell not going to take the blame for keeping my mouth shut or not keeping it shut, either one."

Thelma made wailing noises in the background. Vic had the grace to flush. "Okay. I shouldn't have said it." It was his version of an apology, delivered in clipped, imperious tones. Infuriating bastard. But then, with one of those weary gestures—could they be calculated?—that made Martin feel sorry for him, he rubbed his hand along the side of his face and turned back to Thelma.

"It's late. Come on, dear. Don't cry any more. We must go home."

Her chin trembled. "Vic, I didn't tell you, I took all the housekeeping money, and now it's gone. . ." By some miracle she still had her purse; she fumbled in it and drew out an empty billfold.

"It doesn't matter. Never mind the money, Thelma." Gently but inexorably, he urged her to her feet.

"All right. You don't have to help me. I'm not drunk. Haven't had a drink in hours. All Martin gave me was coffee." She lurched against the end table and giggled. "Not drunk. Just disorderly."

And scared, thought Martin. Snatching at any delaying tactic in sight, however tenuous or futile. And it was futile: with a resigned air, Vic took her arm again and headed her toward the door. His face gave no indication of what he might be thinking.

"What if I get sick?" she quavered.

"I'll hold your head," said Vic. "Come on. We're going home."

She gave Martin one last, big-eyed, entreating look. He could not get it out of his mind. Hours later he woke up, trying not to remember it, trying to convince himself that there was no reason for her to be afraid of Vic.

chapter 9

Next morning, bright and early, Bob White called Martin for lunch. Not unexpectedly: if he had talked to Thelma he must know about last night's session at Martin's apartment; if he had not talked to her he must be wondering where the hell she was. In either case, Martin would seem to him a likely source of information. And that was all right with Martin, who had similar designs of his own.

When he arrived at the modest French restaurant where they had agreed to meet, he found Bob already there, settled at a table and waiting for him. "Hi, Martin. Good to see you again." The sincere handclasp, the deep voice and consciously engaging smile—all were in good working order. Plus a certain rueful, man-to-man air that Martin had no trouble interpreting.

Sure enough. "I just talked to Thelma," Bob said, as soon as the greetings were out of the way, "so we don't have to do any hemming and hawing. She told me all about last night. Or anyway, enough. I know she let the cat out of the bag, to you and Vic both." He paused to adjust his expression, which he seemed to sense was veering unpleasantly toward the complacent. (Fancies himself as a lady-killer, thought Martin. No doubt figures he's irresistible, him and his profile.) "Naturally it shook me up. I didn't even know she was missing. When I couldn't get her yesterday, I just figured she was out shopping or something. If I'd had any idea she was going on a tear—"

"She was okay when you took her home Wednesday night?"

"Sure she was. It never crossed my mind she wasn't going to stay put. I swear she was okay. We had one or two, I admit it, it wasn't quite the way I told you and Rosemary when I went back to The Peacock after my sketch pad."

"So I gathered. She was waiting for you in the place with the pink piano. It's one of the few details she remembers. After that she more or less blanked out."

"She told me. Blanked out and came to on your doorstep. And that's another thing. Why pick your place? Why not go home? Do you know?"

Martin hesitated a moment. Then he said, "I think she was scared."

"Of Vic, you mean? Scared he'd be sore at her for getting drunk? Listen, he used to hit the bottle pretty hard himself, till she straightened him out. He's a fine one to be blaming her when she gets out of line."

"He didn't act sore." Well, and she hadn't acted drunk so much as exhausted. At least not at first; it was only after Vic's arrival that the staggers and mumbles set in. But then, if drunkenness was to some extent a matter of emotions, it might well have been the grip of fear as much as liquor. "No. I got the feeling she was scared of something else. Something connected with Vic, all right. She didn't want to call him. But we had to let him know where she was, otherwise he'd have called the police. I finally convinced her. Then, when he came over to get her, she tried to stall some more."

"She was scared to go home?" Bill licked his lips. "I mean, scared of Vic?"

"She said not. I asked her, before he got there. I thought maybe they'd had some kind of a scene after she got home Wednesday night and that was what had set her off."

"A scene. A fight? About what was going on with Thelma and me? You think he was already wise to us, before she told him last night?"

"He certainly didn't give that impression. No, I'm sure he was jolted. Good and jolted."

"Jolted," Bob repeated. "What interests me is how mad was he. How much hell is he apt to raise. Thelma didn't really go into that part of it."

"He didn't beat her up, if that's what you mean. Actually, he seemed to take it fairly calmly once he got over the first shock." True enough; it wasn't the infidelity angle that was responsible for Martin's night of dire forebodings, his feeling of having thrown her to the wolves, his relief when he called her this morning and heard her voice, remote but composed: yes, she was all right now, poor Martin, she hoped he would forgive her. What had he feared? Well, the same thing Bob feared—physical violence. Only for a different reason. Waiting for her to answer the phone he had conjured up an image of Thelma dead, murdered as Enid had been murdered—not because she was unfaithful but because she knew too much, sometimes drank too much, might have talked too much. But she couldn't know for sure, any more than Martin could! If there were any holes in Vic's alibi the police would have found them. Her facts must be as flimsy as Martin's, and facts were what counted. Never mind the emotional logic. Even so, it would be awkward for Vic if, in a moment of drunken disloyalty, she had spilled out her secret fears and fancies. Had she or hadn't she? Martin ought to be able to find some way of prying the answer out of Bob White. Or whatever his name was.

Apparently he had been busy with a different train of thought, namely, the preservation of his own precious petty skin. "Maybe he's saving his strength for me," he was saying. "Well, he'll have to catch me first."

"Yes, he will. Have you moved yet? I don't think you told me where your new place is."

"I'm not in it yet. A hitch in the paint job. It was supposed to be all set for this week end, but now I don't know. Ah, here we are. Food." He watched, in an abstracted way, as the waiter served their orders. "If I sound like a coward, okay, that's what I am. Put yourself in my place. Would you want to tangle with Vic Holm?"

"What makes you think he's such a dangerous character?" Martin asked, and for a moment they looked straight at each other. Bob's face was motionless, wary. But then his eyes slid away; he grinned a little.

"He's bigger than me," he said. "The way I look at it, anybody bigger than me is dangerous."

"You should have thought of that before you started playing around with his wife."

"True, true. On the other hand, how was I to know she was going to pull this confession act? And for no good reason. That's what gets me. Nobody was bugging her. Nobody pushed her into it."

"I suppose I did, in a way," Martin said. "Pushed her into telling me, I mean. Not Vic. That was her idea. But she had already given the show away at The Peacock, getting so rattled and giving out with the mythical murals business. So when she turned up missing I naturally assumed she'd been off somewhere with you—"

"So help me." Bob disposed of a forkful of veal and, chewing fervently, raised his right hand. "I took her home Wednesday night and that was the last I saw or heard of her till this morning."

"Okay. I believe you. After all, if you'd been off on a binge with her you wouldn't have had the time or energy for your little chat with Hazel Nicholson."

"Oh. She told you, did she? I lost your office phone number," said Bob easily. "Awfully nice woman. So anyway, getting back to Thelma. . ."

"There's nothing to get back to, really. That's it. I don't know if she meant it or not, but she said she didn't want to see you again."

"She meant it all right," said Bob without regret. Rather jauntily, in fact. He caught Martin's eye on him, and added, "Look, I'm sorry it's over. It was great while it lasted. But I never had any illusions about its lasting forever. I'm no home-wrecker. The last thing I wanted was to make trouble between her and Vic. She knew that."

"I should hope so," Martin said. But sometimes, when a woman was as vulnerable as Thelma, she managed to convince herself that even the sorriest little affair was love immortal. It didn't seem possible that she could have looked at Bob and seen anything but the weak, shallow opportunist he was. Yet if she had, it would explain the cheerful way he was accepting the end. Fun and games, yes. Intensity, no. More than he had bargained for. Made him nervous.

"I don't really understand Thelma," he was saying, and for once his candor seemed genuine. "Hell, for all I know, the only reason she took up with me was to get back at Vic. That could be the reason she told him, too. Because the circuit wouldn't be complete until he knew, the way she knew about him and Enid."

Ah yes, Enid. Her name had a way of cropping up in any conversation with Bob White. He was proceeding warily. "I can't help wondering whether it was really all over with those two or whether— You ought to know, as good a friend of Enid's as you were."

"That doesn't make me an authority on her personal affairs," said Martin curtly. If, by refusing to be pumped, he was forfeiting his own chances of pumping Bob—all right, so be it. He had no stomach for such a deal, now that he was faced with it. "The question is, not who was having an affair with Enid, but who killed her. Isn't it? So unless you're suggesting that Vic—"

"Who, me?" Bob leaned back and lit a cigarette. "With an alibi like his? Don't be silly. What's good enough for the police is good enough for me. A double-barrelled alibi, no less. Oh no, I wasn't suggesting a thing. Any more than you were." Again their eyes met, and a smile crept slyly across Bob's face. It sickened and died under Martin's glare. But it had been there, it was still there for Martin, and would be from now on—of all Bob's expressions the unforgettable one, the essence of the fellow himself.

It was also what made Martin follow him when they left the restaurant.

He made no conscious decision to do so. In fact, he was a little surprised to discover that was what he was doing. If Bob had hailed a cab, or made for the subway, or caught a bus, Martin would in all probability have turned around and gone prosily back to the office.

But Bob walked. Downtown on Lexington, and behind him, like a toy pulled on a string, walked Martin. The lunchtime crowds made it irresistibly easy. All he had to do was dawdle or speed up, depending on the traffic lights, and preserve a comfortable chunk of humanity as insulation between him and his quarry. The trail took an eastward turn in the upper Thirties, the people thinned out, and at Third Avenue Martin decided he would be better off on the downtown side of the street and crossed over. He matched his pace to Bob's, which was brisk and purposeful, like that of a man on his way home. Yes, that must be where he was going; in the middle of the block he stopped at a cleaning shop and picked up a couple of suits.

Beginner's luck. It went smooth as silk all the way. Between the cleaner's and the corner Bob slowed down, fumbling for his keys; Martin crossed the street at his leisure (even the traffic lights cooperated) and eureka, the end of the trail, Bob's undisclosed address was undisclosed no longer.

For what the information was worth. Having watched Bob let himself into the basement apartment, Martin just stood there—at his shrewdly safe distance—feeling letdown and rather ridiculous. Now that the excitement of the chase was over, he wondered what its point had been. Certainly not any more conversation with Bob.

Martin knew an impasse when he saw one, and that was what he had seen at lunch. Well then, what?

At least he could walk past the house and take a closer look at it. Its façade was of dingy, lumpy, weather-streaked stucco, with door and wood trim that had long ago, too long ago, been painted turquoise blue. The street-floor apartments were professional, semi-professional: there was a chiropractor's sign, and a dressmaker's. Combined office and living quarters.

And then there was the sign in the window of Bob's basement apartment. "Studio," it read. "Layout—Lettering—Creative Design." Below, in smaller letters, appeared the name. "Robert Black."

Martin was actually all the way past before it registered. The name was not "Robert White." It was "Robert Black." He took a second look to make sure. Thelma's voice came back to him, breathlessly performing the introductions at The Peacock. Bob—White.

It was typical of her, he thought as he headed back for the office. In a freewheeling way, it was appropriate that she should turn Black into White. Or try to. It would take more than a switch in names to sweeten the smell of that guy. How she could ever have taken up with him. . . Anyway, it was over now. If she had to go on a binge to shuck him off, okay, it was worth it.

Even if in her cups she had talked too much, blurted out what she suspected—what Martin suspected she suspected—about Enid's death?

All afternoon the question nagged at him, persistent as a low-grade toothache. He could not ignore it, any more than he could stop spinning his mental wheels in futile review of his own performance at lunch. What he had said, opposed to what he should have said. What opportunities he had failed to see, and saw now with belated brilliance. A busy afternoon: between bouts of rewriting the lunch scene, he examined the possibility—always present with him—that his imagination might be working overtime and that what had looked like skulduggery on Bob's part was nothing very sinister, after all, but only the kind of curiosity known as morbid. Lots of people reacted that way to murder, whether or not they knew the victim. And Bob had known Enid. Known of her.

The curiosity was there, all right. If any further proof were needed, Martin found it when he got home from work. At the street door he met Mrs. Klein setting out with her dog Bubbles for their pre-dinner walk. She was a dim little old soul, spry in her sneakers, dowdy in the gray silk raincoat she wore all summer long, regardless of the weather. Sometimes she interrupted the running conversation she carried on with herself or Bubbles to compliment Martin on "the posies" in his garden; at other times she passed by without noticing either him or his greeting. Tonight she was in touch with the outside world.

"How are you, Mr. Shipley? We were just admiring your posies. So pretty. Such a pleasure. As I said to the young man this morning, it's the little things that make all the difference. I thought I'd put in a good word, you know, in case he felt nervous about taking it."

Martin smiled and waited. It did not pay to rush Mrs. Klein, or try to pin her down.

"I'm not the least bit nervous myself. Bubbles is a wonderful watchdog. I never have to worry with him around. All the same, I'd rather it was rented again. And he was such a nice young man. So nice and polite."

"Oh. A prospective tenant," said Martin. At the

thought of somebody else in Enid's place, he felt a pang of unreasonable resentment. "He was looking at Miss Baxter's apartment?"

"So friendly. After the real estate agent showed it to him we had a little chat. Bubbles and I were just going out. We met them in the hall. As I say, I thought I'd put in a good word. Not that he seemed to feel nervous, but some people might."

"Maybe he didn't know about Miss Baxter."

"They'll redecorate, of course. And I could tell, the terrace appealed to him. He's like you, he likes posies. Poor girl, so did she. I heard the footsteps, you know. Somebody running down the stairs that night. They kept asking me and asking me, but all I could tell them was just footsteps running, and of course Bubbles barking, the way he always does, a wonderful watchdog. Nobody gets past him." She and Bubbles exchanged a look of mutual admiration; he uttered a muted yelp to prove her point, and waggled his portly rear end. "Though generally speaking it's a quiet house, as I told the young man. Very quiet. She didn't have a lot of company."

"He asked about her?"

"It was in the paper. The address and all. Naturally I had no intention of bringing it up. He saw it in the paper. Her name caught his eye because he knows some friends of hers, you see. That's why he was so interested, he thought I might have seen them. And maybe I did, but I'm afraid I don't pay much attention." She peered at Martin apologetically, as she had no doubt peered at the nice young man this morning. "It didn't matter, of course. He just thought I might know them by sight. We had quite a little chat about her. Naturally he was interested."

"Naturally," said Martin. "What did he look like?"

"He didn't seem to feel the least bit nervous about it. Such a nice young man. Life must go on, he said. Terrible, a terrible thing, but life must go on. It's too bad he couldn't have talked to you instead of me. I didn't really know her that well. But you could have told him all about her. It would be so nice for you if he takes it. Another young man in the house. You'd have so much in common."

"I'm sure we would."

"The posies and all." Her gaze wandered off, as it so often did. Bubbles, whose attention span was perfectly attuned to hers, tugged at his leash. They started down the walk, with one accord slipping away into the hazy private world they shared. But before she lost contact entirely, Mrs. Klein had a final message. It drifted back to Martin like a wisp of smoke: "Such a nice-looking young man. Especially from the side. Like John Barrymore."

chapter 10

"He's up to something," said Rosemary. They were having dinner at The Peacock, and Martin had just finished his report on Bob White/Black. "Something about Enid, I mean. He's pumped everybody now. You, me, Mother, Mrs. Klein. Thelma too, I suppose. That's carrying idle curiosity too far. It's got to be something more. You think so too, or you wouldn't have followed him home."

Martin fidgeted with his coffee cup and tried to look like a man who was holding back nothing. It wasn't easy; his account to Rosemary had been artfully abridged to include all the facts and none of his own private unsubstantiated theories. It would have been safer to skip the whole subject. But impossible: she already knew, from their phone conversation this morning, that Thelma had turned up on his doorstep, and that he had a lunch date with Bob. Besides, he wanted to tell her, he had cherished the hope that with her fresh, straightforward eye she might spot some perfectly obvious angle—missed by him; he frequently failed to see the woods for the trees—that would reduce his theories to nonsense.

It wasn't working out that way. If the accusatory tone of her last remark was any indication, what she had spotted with her fresh, straightforward eye was the fact that Martin was holding out on her. And that crack about pumping Thelma too. That sounded as if she might be veering uncomfortably close to his own angle of vision.

"What's he after?" she persisted. "What's he trying to prove? It's not as if he and Enid were friends, or even acquaintances. Enemies? Could that be it?"

"How do you mean, enemies?"

"Well, supposing he made a play for her, and she brushed him off. She wouldn't bother to be tactful about it, you know, not Enid, so it's been eating on him all these years—"

"All these years? When did this happen?"

"Back in Philadelphia. He's never forgotten. It still rankles. So then he finds out she's in New York. From Thelma. Thelma could have told him. Anyway, he finds out, goes to see her, and. . . Martin." Rosemary's voice dropped; her eyelashes worked overtime. "Martin, he could be the one that killed her!"

"Sure," said Martin. "And the reason he's going around pumping everybody is that he's forgotten the details. Wants to refresh his memory." No need to be all that sarcastic, he thought, and reached for her hand. "Never mind. It was a great idea, I only wish it made sense."

"I'm not so sure it doesn't." Her fingers intertwined trustingly in his: a very pleasant arrangement. "It's the kind of weird thing murderers do. Like returning to the scene of the crime. Actually, the part he seemed most interested in was whether or not Enid and Vic were back together again. And that would fit."

"Would it?"

"Sure. Because it was on account of Vic that she brushed him off four years ago. Or so he figures. And he has this compulsion to know if it was Vic again, the second time around. He has to blame somebody, see. It would never occur to him that she was brushing him off for himself alone." After a moment's silence, she returned to her original tack. "There has to be some connection between him and Enid. Something he knows about her, or suspects, or— Could it be something he picked up from Thelma, do you suppose?"

Martin closed his eyes. He tried to keep his voice light. "Here we go again. A great idea a minute."

"All right. But it could be. I still think she may have known about Enid and Vic, that the affair wasn't over. Even if she didn't know for sure, she'd be worried, good and worried. Anybody would be, with a husband as attractive as he is."

"Okay. He's attractive. And maybe Thelma knew. And told Bob. I suppose that's what you're getting at. What of it?"

"I don't know exactly. If he wanted to do Vic some dirt, he could tell the police. They don't like having people lie to them, even when it's about something that doesn't particularly matter."

"Sounds pretty farfetched to me," said Martin. "I can see Bob as a trouble maker, all right, but he's also a coward. I doubt if he'd have the nerve."

"Well, he's up to something," Rosemary repeated stubbornly. "The least we can do is try to find out what.

We've got his address now, and his real name. What are we waiting for?"

"You mean just barge in on him? Now?"

"Why not? If he's really going to move, now's the time." She broke up the pleasant hand arrangement and reached for her purse.

"Yes, but how are we going to— Look, Rosemary, he's a cagey guy. I didn't get anywhere with him at lunch."

"You didn't have me with you," she pointed out. "It's no use trying to figure anything out in advance. We have no idea what tack he's going to take. We'll simply have to play it by ear."

"Now just a minute. I can tell you one tack he's going to take. He's going to ask how the hell I knew where to find him."

"Tell him you got it out of Thelma. That's if you insist on lying. Personally, I don't see anything wrong with telling him the truth—that the name sounded phoney right from the start, and then when he acted so peculiar at lunch, so cagey and all, you decided to follow him and see what was what. After all, he's the one with things to explain. Not you. You've got nothing to hide."

"Be that as it may," Martin murmured. He had to admit, the idea was appealing, in a bold, naive way. It might even work. Approached in this forthright fashion, caught completely off guard—as he almost certainly would be—Bob might actually be surprised into explaining what he was up to. And if Martin's theory turned out to be right?

Well, the test must come some time. He could not just go on harboring his hunch—that Thelma shared his suspicions of Vic and had let them slip to Bob—without ever knowing whether it was true or false. He could not go on harboring his suspicions forever, either; sooner or later he had to know whether or not Vic had indeed been involved in Enid's death as well as her life. For his own satisfaction: no matter what he did with the knowledge. And promise or no promise: he had made no commitment about discovering the truth for himself.

He had to start somewhere. Why not here and now? Well, because. . .

He stared across at Rosemary, shocked by the strangeness and strength of what he was feeling. This was none of her business, it was Vic's and his, an intensely personal thing between the two of them, nobody's business but theirs.

She recapped her lipstick and snapped her compact shut. "Ready?" she asked. "Come on. Let's go."

"Rosemary, I don't think—"

"Listen, Martin. You can sit here and search your soul for the rest of the night if you want to. Or you can come with me. Because I'm going up there to Bob's. With you or without you. Take your choice." She stood up, eyes snapping, ready to switch her neat little rump out of there and up to Bob's.

She meant it. There was nothing to do but go with her.

The cab ride uptown was not sociable. Rosemary sat as far away from him as she could get, and kept her eyes trained on the back of the cabbie's head. Her profile looked purposeful, righteous, and contemptuous of soul searchers. Fortunately she was not a mind reader, or she would have been even more contemptuous: Martin was sustaining himself with the thought that Bob might not be there.

He was, though. And he already had a visitor. The sound of voices reached them through the open window of Bob's basement apartment; against the blind they could see two shifting shadows.

"Are they quarreling?" whispered Rosemary. She had set out, bold as a lion, down the half dozen steps leading to the basement door. Now she hesitated, wide-eyed and nervous.

"Sounds like it to me," said Martin. They stood side by side, listening. The voices were not loud, but there was a disturbing quality about them, a throb of underground violence. Furthermore, they were both familiar, the visitor's as well as Bob's.

"It's Vic, isn't it?"

Martin nodded. So of course it was a quarrel: the only kind of conversation possible between those two. The subject of the quarrel was what mattered.

Bob seemed to be trying a shaky kind of bluster. "Listen, you, don't try anything with me or I'll. . ." It was exasperating, the way his voice fluctuated, blurting and fading like a faulty sound track. And Martin did not trust his own ears; they were so strained to catch the name of Enid that they might hear it whether or not it actually turned up.

Vic sounded ominously pleasant: "You do that. Go right ahead. I dare you to. No? I thought not. That would be cutting off your nose to spite your face, wouldn't it? Remember, I've got a thing or two to tell myself. You miserable little bastard, trying to bluff me. . ."

There was an indistinct mumble from Bob. Sure enough, Enid's name leapt out at Martin. Seemed to leap out.

"Listen, you." Vic again, goading, bullying. "You and your methods. I've got mine too, and so help me, if I find out you ever so much as—"

"I didn't! You can't hang a thing on me, I can prove—"

The voices tangled unintelligibly. The shadows on the window blind suddenly shifted, in a menacing way. A scuffle of feet, a meaty smack, a muffled crash.

"He's killing him," gasped Rosemary. She was clinging to Martin's arm. "What'll we do? Don't go down there, Martin, he's killing him!"

"That's just a sample," Vic said, softly and viciously. "You'll get worse than that if you don't stay the hell away from Thelma. And from me too. Don't mess around. Understand? Just don't mess around."

The door flew open, even before Martin rang the bell. Beyond Vic's furious face and his solid, formidable bulk, they could see Bob propped against the overturned drawing board, his head hanging down, blood dripping from his chin.

"What's going on here?" Martin asked. The policeman's phrase, but without the ring of authority. It sounded as silly as he felt. Bob lifted his head and peered dully; Vic, after one arrogant glance at him and Rosemary, made as if to walk right past them, preferably over them.

But then he changed his mind. "What are you doing here, if you don't mind my asking? The way I heard it, you didn't know where Bob lived. Thought his name was White. How come you didn't say so last night, if you knew—"

"I didn't. I had lunch with him today and trailed him home."

Out of the corner of his eye he saw Bob's jaw drop, then with a resigned air he returned to mopping up his chin. A pathetic sight, at least to Rosemary; she went over to him. "Here, let me help you. Where's a towel?"

Martin and Vic stayed where they were, face to face at the door. "You trailed him home. I see. You just for the hell of it trailed him home. Do you often do things like that?"

"No. Do you often beat guys up?"

"Only when they start fooling around with my wife." A ringing husbandly statement, if Martin ever heard one. Vic delivered it with bravado, and watched to see how it went over. Well, it didn't. Not with Martin. His expression must have indicated as much, for Vic was falling back on the tried and true best defense. "That still doesn't explain what you're doing here now. Another sudden irresistible impulse, I suppose?"

"You can suppose anything you like," Martin said coldly. "I see no reason why I should explain—"

"Oh, stop being so huffy, Martin." Rosemary paused in her ministrations to the wounded long enough to toss this back over her shoulder. "We're here because we wanted to find out what he was up to, snooping around, asking everybody about Enid."

After a second of resounding silence Bob mumbled, "Who, me?"

"Of course you. You've been pumping everybody. Martin, me, Mother, even poor old Mrs. Klein."

"Mrs. who? Who's she?" asked Vic.

"Yeah, who's she?" echoed Bob. "I never—"

"You know perfectly well who she is," said Rosemary severely. "Come on, I'll help you clean up." She hustled him off to the bathroom. There was a businesslike sound of rushing water.

"Enid?" said Vic in a low voice. Almost as if they were

conspirators, Martin thought; as if they were teetering together on the brink of that intensely personal thing between them that was none of Rosemary's business. Instinctively he shrank back—not now, not here, not yet—while Vic waited and watched.

"Enid," he said in the same low voice Vic had used. "She's in this, somehow or other. It's not just Thelma you were fighting about. Bob knows something—"

"He knows about Enid and me, that we were back together again," Vic said quickly. (Is this the way you want it? We don't jump now? Later?) "Suspects it, rather. God knows how he got on to it, or why he should care, one way or the other. Except that he's a trouble maker, a rat from way back."

"You did know him, then, in Philadelphia?"

"I knew who he was. His name was familiar." He paused a moment, curiously; when Martin made no comment he went on, with growing assurance. "I'm not sure I would have recognized him if I'd just met him cold. I am sure I don't want him messing around, stirring up trouble, getting Thelma in a twitch. That's what set her off the other night, him and his big mouth."

"I see. You threatened to do some talking yourself, if he didn't lay off. What was all that about?"

"Principally bluff," said Vic with his candid air. "I figured it was safe as long as I didn't get down to specifics. A rat like Bob is bound to have at least one smelly little episode in his past. Besides, he's a coward, one of those guys you can't resist bullying. Anyway, I can't."

The next moment nurse and patient emerged from the bathroom. "Of course it was you," Rosemary was saying irritably. "Mrs. Klein told Martin about it, that's how we know. He recognized you from her description. No use your denying it."

But that was what Bob persisted in doing. His hair was slicked down now, and the dull look was gone from his eyes. Except for a puffy lip and a plum-colored bruise on his jaw, he was back to normal. And sticking to his "who, me?" routine. Never heard of Mrs. Klein. Hadn't pumped her or anybody else about Enid. Couldn't imagine where they had gotten such an idea. Naturally he'd been interested, having known Enid, known of her. Was it his fault she was on everybody's mind?

"You mentioned her tonight to Vic!" Rosemary burst out. Her face was pink with frustration. "I heard you, I'm positive I heard you!"

"Tonight?" Bob lifted his shoulders, spread his hands helplessly. Martin had noticed before how his eyes kept shifting toward Vic, in apprehensive little bids for approval; now it was an open, insolent look, and with it came that unforgettably sly smile. "I give up. It's your turn, Vic. Maybe you can convince her."

"I never argue with a lady," said Vic promptly, and gave Rosemary the old razzle-dazzle smile. "If she heard it, she heard it. Good night. An ice pack might help. And don't forget what I told you."

There was no danger of that; he had accomplished his mission, and they all knew it. Evidently even Rosemary had given up all hope of getting anything out of Bob. "Let's go too," she said, and they followed Vic out the door and up the half dozen steps to the street.

He said good night as cheerfully and easily as if they were parting after a nice friendly get-together. But Rosemary had one more question. "How did *you* get hold of his real name and address? Did you pry it out of Thelma?"

"Beat it out of her, you mean? Like the brute I am? No, as it happens, I didn't have to. I remembered this quirk of Thelma's and figured it out on my own."

"This quirk?"

"She has a way of speaking in opposites. Especially when she's nervous. She'll say up for down, left for right, back for front. White for Black. Once I remembered that, it was elementary. All I had to do was look him up in the phone book. Good night."

Off he went. And after a moment off they went, in the opposite direction. They found a cab at the corner and rode uptown—Rosemary wanted to go straight home, no nightcap, thank you—in almost complete silence. Not unsociably this time; they sat close together, holding on to each other's hands. But thinking their separate thoughts. How separate only Martin knew. For his were focused on Vic and the private showdown they both knew was impending, the moment when they would shuck off subterfuge and take the perilous jump into truth.

Was it possible that Rosemary sensed he was still holding out on her? She was awfully damn quiet. And when they reached her mother's apartment she did not ask him in. At the door she said, in a subdued little voice, "It was a stupid idea, wasn't it? It wouldn't have worked, even if Vic hadn't been there. People don't tell you things just because you ask. Especially when it's a question of—of murder." She shivered. "And it is. Murder. It does make sense, what I said before, about Bob. You see it now too, don't you? Just the way he denied it to Vic—"

Bob. She thought it was Bob. They had overheard the same conversation; and come up with two entirely different translations. It was either very grim or very funny, Martin couldn't decide which.

"I'll call you tomorrow," he said, and kissed her gently. "Maybe we can dope it all out then."

chapter 11

"No egg?" cried Hazel. "But it's Saturday!" She set the glass skillet back on the stove and gave her daughter a sharp look. Week end breakfasts were a tradition with them, and a treat: one of the few occasions when there was time for Hazel to revert to her native, country domesticity; time for them both to linger over extra cups of coffee and have a nice little gossip.

"I'm not hungry," Rosemary said wanly. She slid into her side of the breakfast nook and leaned her chin on her hand. Hazel decided she looked peaked.

"I didn't hear you come in last night. What time was it?"

"I don't know. Not late."

"Good time?"

Rosemary shrugged.

"You and Martin had a fight. Is that it?"

"Of course we didn't have a fight. For Pete's sake, Mom. Light somewhere and stop hovering!"

Stung into silence (hovering!) Hazel sat down too. She took another muffin and brooded about Martin Shipley. It was these nice quiet ones that did the damage. "Of course" they hadn't had a fight; nothing so vulgar or wholesome as that. She remembered the wolfish way he had smiled, that first afternoon, when poor innocent Rosemary had blurted out the business about his wife. His wife! Apprehension clutched her. How could she have forgotten, even for a moment, the ominous question of Martin's past? Yes, forgotten, brushed it aside, dismissed it as if it were nothing out of the ordinary, the kind of harmless scrape any boy could get into. A possible wife-murderer, that was all, and she had let him loose with Rosemary, who was a babe in the woods, never mind her sophisticated airs, and who now sat there moping and looking peaked and not eating her breakfast.

Their eyes met, and Rosemary said, with a pathetic little quaver in her voice, "The fact is, Mom, last night kind of scared me."

Hazel's knife clattered against her plate. She grabbed wildly for Rosemary's hand. "Baby! Tell me! What did he do to you?"

"Who?"

"That Martin of course. Who else? Oh, I could kick myself, I should never have—"

"Honestly, Mom! Simmer down. What's the matter with you this morning? Martin didn't do anything to me. Nobody did. Get your mind off rape and listen."

It hadn't been on rape so much as murder, and that—Hazel realized as she obediently simmered down and listened—was what had frightened Rosemary about last night. Enid's murder. It had hit her in a different, harder way. From the beginning, of course, it had been an indisputable fact. There was nothing hypothetical about it, as there was about the death of Martin's wife; it could not be glossed over as an accident. The only possible spot for a bit of glossing over (and Hazel and Rosemary had both snatched at it) was the identity of the murderer. They could not deny that someone had killed Enid, but they could deny that it was someone who knew her. It was more comfortable to believe in a panicky, anonymous intruder; it somehow kept murder at manageable arm's length. Last night had all but destroyed Rosemary's faith in the intruder. By the time she was through with her story, Hazel herself was aware of a few inner quakes and crumblings. But she was not about to admit it.

"Now look here, Rosemary," she said at last. "You're letting your imagination run away with you. Sure, Bob could have made a play for Enid, could even have killed her, I suppose. But there's not one single solid fact to prove it. No evidence that he ever saw her here in New York, or knew her better than he claims, or anything. All you know for sure is that he's been asking a lot of questions about her, and he had a fight with Vic. Who had a perfectly good reason for taking a poke at him, aside from Enid."

"They weren't just fighting about Thelma," Rosemary said mulishly. "It was about Enid too. Bob's mixed up in it somehow. If he didn't kill her himself he knows something—"

"Something Vic doesn't want him to tell," Hazel finished for her. "That's what you're suggesting, isn't it? Something that would implicate Vic."

"Well. Well, I guess so. Or maybe Thelma?"

"Or maybe Thelma. Something that would implicate

one of the Holms." She let that sink in. She was feeling better by the minute; there was nothing like a few blunt statements to straighten things out. "And that really is pretty farfetched, Rosemary. I simply can't believe the police wouldn't have gotten on to it too, if there was anything to get on to. They checked the Holms' story backwards and forwards, and didn't find any holes in it. It's not just their story, remember. That Mrs. McGrath was visiting them the night Enid was killed. It's her story, too."

"I know it. I know the Holms couldn't have killed her. And I know I can't prove anything about Bob. All the same, that fight last night, it was about Enid. It was, it was!"

"But not necessarily about her death. Look. Why couldn't they have been talking about her affair with Vic? It would be like Bob to bring that up, under the circumstances. You know. Throwing it in Vic's face that he hasn't always been so faithful himself. That's certainly the angle Bob was working on when he paid his little call on me."

"Yes, but Mom, the very fact that he paid his little call on you means— Well, why would he bother? What's it to him if Vic and Enid had gotten together again here in New York?"

"Spite," said Hazel promptly. "Chances are he knew Thelma was about ready to chuck him, if she hadn't already, and he was looking for a way to get even with her and Vic both, make trouble between them. There are people like that and if you ask me he's one of them. Bob White, Black, Whatever." It was quite a convincing argument, at least to her own ears. She pressed on energetically. "Honestly, Rosemary, doesn't it make more sense? I know you were there and I wasn't, but— How about Martin? What does he make of all this?"

"I don't know," said Rosemary with a queenly air. "We didn't discuss it."

"Didn't discuss it! Why on earth not?"

Rosemary maintained a regal silence. But her chin trembled slightly, as if she might be on the verge of tears. That Martin. Fight or no fight, something had gone wrong. Didn't discuss it! Why, it was against human nature, they must not even be on speaking terms. And just as well too, with that big black shadow in Martin's past. If Hazel had a hollow, grieving feeling—yes, all right, she had—it was on Rosemary's account, poor child, but of course she would bounce back, all it took was time.

She had no sooner settled the matter in her mind, more or less satisfactorily, than the phone rang: Martin, she could tell from Rosemary's voice; obviously very much on speaking terms. The joys of motherhood, Hazel thought, in helpless agitation. What did she do now? Forbid Rosemary to see him again? Ha! Demand from Martin a yes-or-no answer: did you or did you not murder your wife? There was a limit, even to Hazel's bluntness. Yet to do nothing, to stand by, silent and inert, while. . .

"Thelma's invited us for lunch!" Rosemary called from the hall. "Martin says she asked him to bring us. Shall I tell him okay, Mom?"

A reprieve. Hazel's heart bobbed up like a balloon. More than a reprieve. A heaven-sent opportunity to meet Thelma Holm and judge her at first hand; to take another look at Martin, a cold, hard, maternal look this time, no nonsense about whether or not she happened to like him personally; and incidentally, to get his version of last night. That too, of course.

"Wonder how she happened to ask us," she said, when Rosemary came back, looking considerably less peaked.

"Vic's working—he puts in a lot of overtime—and I think she gets lonesome. She doesn't seem to have many friends here, they're all in Philadelphia. That's probably why she took up with Bob. Lonesomeness. Otherwise I can't see it, he doesn't seem her type at all. Martin said she sounded fine. Gay as a lark. Maybe she's celebrating Liberation Day from Bob."

"Does she know what happened last night?"

"She didn't mention it. So don't you, Mom, you keep your mouth shut, will you, for once in your life?"

It was the kind of slur Hazel was used to. She ignored it. "You know, Rosemary, I bet Dennis could give me a line on Bob Black, if I wanted to call him."

"Dennis?"

"You know. Enid worked with him when she was in Philadelphia. I sent her to him. He's lived there forever. Knows all kinds of people. And he's gossipy as an old hen. What do you think? It might be worth a try."

It was indeed worth a try. She didn't get Dennis right away; no answer at first, then a busy signal, at last—by this time they were ready and waiting for Martin to pick them up—Dennis' light, vivacious voice came on the line. In accordance with Rosemary's instructions, Hazel worked the subject around to Bob Black by an indirect route. After that she listened. Just as she hung up, the doorbell rang: Martin, on the dot of twelve thirty, with a cab waiting.

So she wound up giving them her report on Bob Black

while they rode downtown to have lunch with Thelma Holm. There was no time to sort it out in her own mind first; not with Rosemary champing at the bit. Out it came, boom: "He's Lulu McGrath's brother. A ne'er-do-well, Dennis says, can't keep a job, never pays his bills, always getting into some kind of hot water and hollering for good old big sister Lulu to fish him out. She used to do it, all the time, till her husband got fed up and laid it on the line. Either she washed her hands of brother Bob or she found herself another husband. This was a couple of years ago, after Lulu had wangled a job for Bob in one of the McGrath enterprises. There are a lot of them. He's loaded. Dennis doesn't know exactly what happened, it was hushed up, but McGrath blew his top and booted Bob out, and nobody's seen or heard of him since."

"Including Lulu, I suppose?" Martin's voice, coming from the other corner of the cab, beyond Rosemary, sounded detached; he seemed to be gazing off into space.

"Especially Lulu. Naturally she's not going to break up her marriage for the sake of a black sheep brother. She came up the hard way, she knows a good thing when she's got it. Not many girls from the wrong side of the tracks are lucky enough to snag a McGrath."

"It connects him with the Holms, though," Rosemary pointed out. "How about Enid? Did she know Bob too, better than anybody's saying?"

"Not as far as Dennis knows. I certainly can't see her bothering with a fellow like Bob. Can you?"

"I can't see Thelma bothering, either. But she did."

"Well, but you said yourself, she's lonely. A lonely, neglected wife, and a semi-alcoholic. . ." Hazel had a confused feeling that she was floundering; in some obscure way the discovery of Bob's identity seemed to undermine the comforting, convincing argument she had evolved over the breakfast table. "It's not the same at all. And anyway. What's the difference how well he knew Enid, or whose brother he is? I can't see that it proves anything about the set-to he had with Vic last night. Do you, Martin?" That proved how rattled she was, that she should be appealing to Martin. "Rosemary's got this notion they weren't fighting about Thelma at all—"

"You're twisting it around, Mom! It was partly about Thelma, of course. But it was about Enid too. You know it as well as I do, Martin, whether you'll admit it or not!"

So there they were, both of them, appealing to Martin, and he continued to gaze off into space, shutting them out, refusing to commit himself. It came to Hazel that this was what had gone wrong between him and Rosemary last night: no quarrel but no discussion either; simply the chill of being shut out, without knowing why or from what. But Martin was miserable too. She saw it in his eyes when he turned toward Rosemary and put his hand over hers.

"Remember what you said last night," he said. "People don't tell you things just because you ask. You were right, they don't. Let's don't ask Thelma, and see what she tells us."

Which didn't strike Hazel as much of an answer. But then he wasn't holding her hand or giving her the soulful-eyes routine. She looked out the window and waited grimly for the tender moment to pass.

"Don't worry," she said as the cab pulled up to the curb. "Rosemary's already warned me about keeping my mouth shut."

"We go up these stairs." Martin guided them past the

store window with its display of trusses and cervical collars. "It's kind of a weird arrangement, isn't it? But they have lots of space, the two top floors to themselves." He pushed the bell, the buzzer promptly sounded, and they started climbing the narrow, dark stairway, which smelled of Vitamin B.

The woman waiting for them at the top was smiling radiantly. Lonely? Neglected? Semi-alcoholic? Not so you could notice it. She was tall and willowy as a girl; standing like that, with her arms outstretched in welcome, she gave an effect of youthfulness and warmth that took Hazel completely by surprise. No one had told her that Thelma Holm was charming. But then it should have been self-evident. Only a charming woman could have held her husband against competition as stiff as Enid.

She had a breathless, impulsive way of talking, jumping from pillar to post, juggling two or three conversational balls at once, bubbling with pleasure in her own party. Such a small party, and made up of people drawn together by such ugly, shocking events. . . Yes, she must be lonely, after all. And her face, when seen close up, showed lines of strain, as if, with no one around to sparkle for, its basic expression would be one of sad bewilderment.

"No cause for alarm, Martin," she said as she handed around a tray of drinks. "I'm back on the ginger ale circuit. You heard about my fall from grace, Mrs. Nicholson? Good, I hoped Martin would tell you, otherwise I probably would, and it's not really very interesting. . . Poor Martin, what a nuisance I made of myself, and you were so good to me. Anybody else would have sent me packing."

"I did," said Martin, smiling. "Don't you remember? I

made you call Vic, and then I sent you home with him, even though you obviously didn't want to go. I worried about it afterwards, you acted so scared."

"Who, me? That's how I am when I get drunk. I never want to go home. I had nothing to be scared of. You saw how Vic was, a perfect lamb about the whole thing." She patted her glossy bangs, and shot a quick glance at each of them in turn. "No point in pretending, is there? I can see everybody knows the worst. Should I be embarrassed? I'm not. It's a relief to me, having it out in the open like this. In a way, that's why I invited you. And I'm very grateful to you for coming. It was Vic's idea, actually. I was upset when he told me about last night, you see. That did embarrass me. Martin and Rosemary being there, I mean. What must you have thought!"

"So Vic said ask us to lunch and find out," said Martin drily.

"Of course not! How could you think— Well, yes, partly." Her laugh rang out, unself-conscious as a child's. "Naturally, I'm curious."

"So were we," said Martin. "And so was Bob. That's why we were there, why I tracked him down in the first place. Because he seemed so extraordinarily curious about Enid."

"I know." Thelma's eyes darkened slightly; there was no other sign that it had given her a turn. (As it had Hazel.) "He started in on me, too, trying to convince me that Vic and—that they were back together again. I know perfectly well it's not true, but all the same it bothered me. That was his point, I guess, he likes getting people stirred up. Especially me. He knew it would send me off on a binge. And it did. He's not really a very nice person, is he?" Her hands moved aimlessly, helplessly.

"You said a minute ago, scared. Well, it's true. Only of course it wasn't Vic I was scared of, it was Bob. I was afraid to go home for fear he'd call me or—something. I couldn't bear the thought of hearing his voice again, not even over the phone. You wouldn't believe how spiteful he can be. Especially about Vic. It's frightening, the way he resents Vic. Almost as if he had a grudge."

That was all Rosemary needed. Up with the head, out with the chin. She was off: "Maybe he did have. Maybe he had a thing about Enid himself, back in Philadelphia, and feels he lost out on account of Vic. He might still have been after her, here in New York. It's not the kind of thing she'd mention to anybody, and neither would he. Certainly not after what happened to her."

Martin groaned. Hazel sighed.

But Thelma said quietly, "I've sometimes wondered myself. It might even be the reason he took up with me. To get even with Vic. He's capable of it. Capable of anything."

"That's going pretty far, isn't it?" said Martin.

"Not too far. Believe me. What a fool I've been, what a fool! The one thing to be said in my favor is that I see it now. Well, and I did have sense enough to know he was lying about Vic and Enid." Did she expect someone to argue with her? No one did. No one spoke at all. After a moment she rushed on. "Oh, I'm so glad it's over! I'm so glad I told Vic about it, the other night at your house, Martin. That's another thing I have to thank you for. I never would have told him, if it hadn't been for you."

"No, I don't suppose you would have," said Martin, in what struck Hazel as a rather odd tone. "As it was, you didn't tell him—or me either—who Bob really is, did you?"

"Oh, you mean the Black-White business. I just—"

"No, I mean the fact that he's Lulu McGrath's brother."

"Oh," she said. She covered her mouth with her hands—ringless, Hazel noticed, not even a wedding band—and shrank back like a smacked child. "Oh dear. I was so ashamed. I thought if I said White instead of Black nobody would ever find out. Only Vic caught on anyway, and now you— Who told you?"

"A friend of Hazel's in Philadelphia. I told you we were curious. Even more so after last night. We got the impression that Vic could make some trouble for Bob too, and would, if he was pushed far enough."

"Oh. Well, there was something a couple of years ago, I don't know exactly what, but it was the last straw as far as Lulu was concerned. I bet Vic doesn't know any more than I do. He must have been bluffing."

"So he said. I must say, it seemed to work."

She smiled, rather proudly, Hazel thought. The female primeval, pleased at being fought over, pleased too at the outcome. "That's why I didn't want Vic to find out, you see. It made it less ignominious, for both of us, to have him think it was nobody he knew. Just an anonymous somebody I'd taken up with when I wasn't entirely myself. I was ashamed to have him find out it was a—a good-for-nothing like Bob Black. Poor Vic, I might at least have picked somebody decent."

"How about poor Bob? He's the one that got socked."

"He had it coming. So did I, if you want my honest opinion. Only I was just foolish, not malicious like Bob. Funny, isn't it? He was doing his best to make trouble between Vic and me, and what he actually did was bring us closer together. There now. That ends today's episode in the Holms' soap opera. Another drink, everybody?"

She sprang up, head tilted, hands lifted in a gesture that for some reason made Hazel think of a magician's flourish. A trick? But everything she had said fit in with the facts, and furthermore with Hazel's own theories, which had seemed so comfortingly logical when she thought of them herself. She was not going to start picking holes in them now. Smiling—as Rosemary and even Martin were smiling—she accepted another drink and resolutely bent her mind to enjoying the party.

The phone rang while they were finishing their coffee and discussing the living room walls. ("I still think murals," Thelma declared, "only not please God Bob Black's.") She looked startled, maybe even panicky, at the peal of the bell, but when she came back from answering it her face was radiant again.

"That was Lulu!" she cried. "They're just back from their cruise, Mac has to get back to Philadelphia, but she's going to stay over till tomorrow, she's just around the corner— No, no, don't go, please stay. It will be such fun. A welcome-back party!"

There was just time, before Lulu's arrival, for her to add, with a shamefaced, pleading air, "You won't mention any of this? About Bob? Because of course Lulu has no idea. . . She never sees him any more, hasn't in at least two years, after that last mess he got into she wrote him off as a bad bet. She doesn't even know he's in New York. So you won't say anything, will you? It would be too terribly embarrassing."

Lulu was a sleek little package of a woman: one of those durable, compact figures; expert maintenance all over the place—ash-blonde hair, flawless teeth, fingernails like perfect, rosy shells. Against her pecan-brown tan her white linen dress was dazzling, not a wrinkle in it. A modest fortune had no doubt been invested in her charm bracelet, another—not so modest—in her diamond. Yet there was something about her that took the curse off all this surface artifice—a quality of basic naturalness that refused to be polished away and that kept Hazel from begrudging her even her shoes, which were bright red, spike-heeled, sling pumps. Lulu's voice was husky and faintly raffish. Her eyes looked out at the world with a kind of zestful, astonished self-mockery, as if she were saying, Hey, look what's happened to little wrong-side-of-the-tracks Lulu, hey, how about that!

Thelma fell on her neck like a lost child restored to home and mother. "I've missed you so. Oh, Lulu, I can't tell you how good it is to have you back!"

Too true, she couldn't tell, thought Hazel. And like as not none of this would have happened if Lulu had been here to keep Thelma on the beam. For that was obviously her role: her manner toward Thelma was definitely managing, affectionate but firm.

"I hope you've been behaving yourself," she said. "How's Vic? Okay? Listen, dearie, you promised me you were going to get to work on this place and get it shaped up while I was away. I expected a transformation, and what do I get? The same old shambles. Six months, and you haven't even finished unpacking! You ought to be ashamed."

"I am," said Thelma, with a flickering half-wink toward her other three guests.

They stayed only a few minutes longer. Such a nice lunch, so nice of Thelma to ask them, so nice to meet Lulu. They must get together again, very soon. Goodbye, goodbye.

They trooped down the stairs, waving and smiling and not saying a single embarrassing word about Lulu's black sheep brother Bob.

chapter 12

Once they reached the street, of course, there was no holding back. Rosemary began it; the gleam in her eye made Martin think of a prosecuting attorney turning the tables on a hostile witness. "Well. Now try and tell me Bob Black had nothing to do with Enid. It's not just in my head. It's in Thelma's, too, the very same idea. I guess that proves it isn't so crazy, after all."

What it proved to Martin—though he refrained from saying so—was that Thelma had a remarkable talent for picking up other people's suggestions and making the most of them. Rosemary's suggestion, in this case, though she seemed to have lost sight of the fact. Not Martin. Indeed, it was during this particular part of the pre-lunch conversation, while Thelma was skillfully scooping up Rosemary's idea and tossing it back as her own, that he had experienced a revelation. Watching Thelma in action, he remembered his own conversation with her Wednesday night, and he saw, with flash-of-lightning clarity, that it was he, not Thelma, who had launched the idea of an affair between her and Bob. The affair that was now an accepted fact, unlikely as the combination had seemed at first glance. To everybody. Thelma herself had stared at him incredulously for a moment before she went off into that fit of hysterical giggles. What relief she must have felt, what gratitude to Martin for handing her this nice simple way of explaining the presence of Bob in her life! Then too there was the ironic touch, the inside-out logic (Thelma's favorite kind) of being most loyal to Vic when she was confessing her infidelity.

For Martin now realized that the key to everything Thelma did was just that: loyalty to Vic. She had pounced on the role of unfaithful wife gladly, gladly. Let everybody think she was a tramp. Just don't let anybody think Vic was a murderer. Better Bob as temporary bedmate than as blackmailer. And trust Bob to pick her as his victim. Unlike Vic, she wasn't bigger than he was; she had neither the strength nor temperament to hit back. Suggestible, easily rattled—she sometimes drank too much, bless her heart—and above all devoted to Vic, ready to protect him no matter what she herself might suspect him of doing. Oh, she was the one, all right, the perfect customer for Bob's modest little racket. As to what he actually had on Vic, it was anybody's guess, thought Martin, pure speculation. The chances were all against Bob's talking now. Thanks to Vic. He knew how to handle rats like Bob; Thelma should have told him the whole story in the first place. But that would have meant admitting her own suspicions. Being loyal to Vic didn't keep her from being scared of him.

No wonder she was in buoyant spirits today. The Holms had squeaked through another tight spot, with only minor abrasions, and closer together than ever. No wonder, either, that she had snatched at the chance, so conveniently offered by Rosemary, to steer suspicion toward Bob, who was guilty of a worse crime than murdering Enid, the rotter, he had tried to make trouble between her and Vic. . .

"I never said it was crazy." Hazel's voice jolted him out of his own private reverie. She sounded defensive, as if Rosemary was making her feel like a hostile witness too, and she shifted uneasily from one space shoe to the other. "All I said was you've got no proof. You still haven't. Just because Thelma happens to agree with you—"

"You heard her. She was scared of Bob herself, scared of what he might do. Spiteful, resentful, capable of anything, she said. Anything. Including murder. She didn't say it in so many words, but that's what she meant. And she knows him, if anybody does."

"Better than his sister?" Martin asked. It was last night all over again; two entirely different translations. He had the same eerie, displaced feeling. "Yes, I suppose you're right, if Lulu hasn't seen him in the past couple of years."

The operative word, for him, was "if." But not for Rosemary. Or Hazel, either; she was saying, with an air of relief at finding one point of agreement, "She's given him up as a bad job too. Just as Dennis said. I'm not denying he's a real no-account."

"He's a lot worse than that, if you ask me." Rosemary looked flushed. Very pretty, and very obstinate. "I think the police ought to know about him. It's different when they ask questions. He'll have to tell them."

It figured. Martin should have known it was coming. But the knot of resistance that tightened inside him had nothing to do with knowing or thinking. It was instinctive. A great big panicky mindless No. Not the police. Not yet. Not before he and Vic had it out between them, the intensely personal thing that was nobody else's business. He said, quite calmly, "Now wait a minute, Rosemary. Before we go to the police—"

"You'll come with me, then?" Her eyes lit up.

"If you go I have no choice. They'll want my version of the fight last night, to see if it checks with yours. No getting out of it."

"No getting out of it," she echoed scornfully. "You'd like to get out of it. Why? Do you think I'm crazy too? Don't you want them to find out who killed Enid?"

Don't answer that question. Pick the easy one. "I don't think you're crazy. You've got a right to your opinion. But so have I, and I think it would be—all wrong to go to the police at this stage of the game." Thin ice. Watch your step. He glanced at Hazel, trying to judge how much of an ally she might prove to be. Her big, plain face showed worry. Uncertainty. A shade of mistrust? Oh Lord, the Joyce business. "I mean, stop and think a minute first."

"Oh sure. Search your soul. Drag your feet. That's you all over. It's a wonder to me you ever get dressed in the morning, what with making up your mind which sock to put on first, and then which shoe—can't have either of them feeling rejected, you know—"

"At least I don't go galloping off without looking where I'm going, or why. The police ought to know about Bob. Okay. Maybe. Let's be good citizens. Let's tell them about Bob. He deserves it. He's no good. A rat. But don't forget if we tell them about Bob it means telling them about Thelma too. I don't see any way of keeping her out of it. Do you?"

She didn't. And she hadn't thought of that side of it before. She gave a little gulp of dismay.

"Oh no," said Hazel, stricken.

"Oh yes. It would all come out. That she sometimes drinks too much. That she was foolish enough to get involved with Bob. Furthermore that there are still those who think her husband was Enid's lover, no matter what he and Thelma told the police before. That too. Once more through the meat grinder for both the Holms. With Bob directing every turn of the handle, and relishing it."

"They'd grind him through, too."

"True. They might even get something out of him. Then again, they might not. Your mother's right, Rosemary, you've got no proof, not even an honest to God connection between Bob and Enid. All you've got so far is a hunch, and I don't think that's enough. I think you ought to wait till—"

She was looking scornful again, half ready to bolt off on her own and leave him to his miserable soul searching. But Hazel put a hand on her arm. "Now calm down, Rosemary. Wait till what?" The look she gave Martin was both hopeful and suspicious. "You're hatching something, Martin. At least it sounds like it to me."

"As a matter of fact, I am." Could he leave it at that? No. He would have to improvise. "Call it a hunch of my own. Something I have to work out by myself. No use telling you about it yet. I have to think it through first, figure out the best way to tackle it."

"Naturally," said Rosemary. "A year or so of preliminary research, I suppose?"

"An hour or so. Sorry to disappoint you."

"Well? And then what?"

"Well. And then I tackle it. I test my hunch, find out if I'm right or wrong. That shouldn't take long, either. And after that. . . One thing I do know. The timing's got to be right. If you go to the police now you'll louse me up.

Be a sport, Rosemary? Give me till tonight, tomorrow morning at the latest. Bob will keep till then. If it turns out I'm way off the track with my hunch, I give you my word, we'll go to work on yours."

She was wavering, he could see, but he did not realize what a total victory he had won until she spoke. "This test of yours. Won't it be dangerous?"

"Dangerous?" It was odd that the question should take him by surprise, odd that he should feel less like Vic's Nemesis than his fellow-conspirator. Surely Rosemary had a point? And such a flattering one; the temptation to play up to it was well-nigh irresistible. "I don't think so, really. Not if I play my cards right."

"Then see that you do," Hazel said, and promptly looked as if she wished she hadn't. "Come on, Rosemary, let's go home and let Martin figure out his tactics."

He hailed a cab for them (no, he was not to come with them; he was to get busy figuring) and they said their goodbyes. "Take care. Be sure to call, won't you?" Rosemary whispered. She gave him a quick kiss. And at the last minute Hazel shook hands with him.

All very nice and ego-building, to use Bob's phrase. But the fact remained that Rosemary had pressured him into committing himself and Vic. They were in for it now; no more dodging or postponing the showdown. Dangerous or not, it was inevitable. Tomorrow morning at the latest. That meant tonight, this afternoon, the sooner the better. He stepped into a sidewalk phone booth, looked up the number of Vic's office, and dialled.

There was no answer. In his mind's eye he saw the Saturday emptiness, the deserted switchboard, one line left open for the benefit of extra-time workers like Vic—who was either not bothering to answer or had already left. Or might never have been there at all: "the office" might be a cover-up term for him, his explanation for the evenings he had spent with Enid, his escape hatch now. The thought conjured up another mental picture, sharp as an etching, of Vic tramping the streets, any streets, in a stupor of sorrow, as Martin himself used to do, after Joyce's death.

But this was the sort of thing he must stop, this imaginary empathy with Vic. There was no basis for it. Two totally different people, two totally different cases. Not comrades. Opponents. He was wasting his time, straying off on these dead-end paths, when he should be marching down the main road with his tactics figured out and his forces marshalled.

There was no help for it: he would have to wait till Vic got home and call him there. With some excuse prepared in advance, in case Thelma or Lulu answered the phone. In the meantime, what? He paused outside the phone booth, remembering Rosemary's scornful references to soul searching. Action, he thought nervously, up and at 'em. Don't just stand there. Do something.

He got on a bus and rode up to Bob's street, partly on impulse, partly because he remembered something else—a notion that had stirred briefly in the underground of his mind while Rosemary was making noises about the police. That threat of hers, which had forced a deadline on him and Vic, had throbbed for a moment with still another potential. Now it was stirring and throbbing again; by the time he reached Bob's house he saw how it could be used as a lever on Bob and, through him, on Vic.

But he was too late. (Typically, Rosemary would have said.) The "Studio" sign was gone from the basement apartment window; the name of Robert Black no longer appeared beside bell or mailbox. Bob had skipped out. Either that mythical new apartment of his wasn't mythical, after all, or—more likely—he wasn't taking any chances on a second visit from Vic.

In his new role of man of action, Martin rang the bell marked Superintendent. Presently the street door opened and a woman stuck her head out. A small head, like a chicken's, with dyed red hair and a pointed nose, perched on top of a withered neck. Her voice was like a chicken's, too, fussy, full of clucks and cackles. "Ain't here any more," she said in answer to Martin's question. "Moved out last night, bag and baggage. Such as it was. Just like that, without giving me notice. Didn't say where he was moving to. Just up and left."

"You mean without paying the rent?"

She really did cackle at that. "Do I look like some kind of a nut? They don't pull that on me. Oh no. They pay in advance, or out they go. Including Mr. Black. You a friend of his?"

"An acquaintance." He was inspired to add, "I know his sister."

"That so? Mrs. Richbitch, to hear him tell it. It's one of the lines they try to pull on me, see, they've all got wealthy connections that are going to put a check in the mail tomorrow. Cuts no ice with me. Though I'll say this much for Mr. Black, his sister looked like she might be the real McCoy." Again she uttered her high-pitched, cracked laugh. "That's a good one. The real McCoy. Because her name's Mc Something, see, Mrs. Mc Something or Other."

"McGrath," said Martin. "She's been here? You've met her?"

"That's it. McGrath. I didn't meet her exactly. Just saw her the once—four, five months ago, soon after he moved in—and he told me afterwards it was her. No kidding, is she loaded like he said?"

"Her husband's wealthy."

"Yeah. He told me. She looked it, all right. You could get his new address from her. He'll keep in touch with her, don't worry, he knows which side his bread is buttered on."

"Yes, I'm sure you're right. I'll call her."

He had nothing to lose by trying, he decided on the way home. He was calmed down now, determined not to overestimate Lulu's visit to her black sheep brother four, five months ago. That didn't mean she knew his present whereabouts, or would admit it if she did. But she was the only lead in sight, his one hope of getting hold of Bob and putting his lever idea to the test. There was even a chance—slim, but still—that the lever would work on Lulu as well as Bob. And he had to call the Holms, anyway, since he had missed Vic at the office. Two out of three, he thought as he dialled the number: it shouldn't be Thelma who answered, but with his luck it probably would be. Okay, he was prepared. He would disguise his voice and ask for Vic.

"Hello?" It was Lulu's husky voice; luck was being a lady, for once. "Oh yes," she said, when he had identified himself. "Thelma's gone out to do some errands, and Vic hasn't come home yet. Can I take a message?"

"Actually, you're the one I wanted to talk to." Martin's mouth went dry, and with it his brain. Dry and blank.

"I'm all ears," said Lulu cheerfully.

"Well. It's about your brother. I'm very anxious to get hold of him."

"You are?" Not so cheerful now. Cautious. Defensive.

"It's a little complicated. I met him, you know. Or did you know?"

Silence. Once more drouth had struck Martin's mind. Then Lulu said, with a show of impatience, "What is all this? I mean, why call me? I never see Bob any more."

"Don't you? That's one of the things I wanted to talk to you about."

"What do you— Listen. Where are you?"

"Home." He gave her the address.

"I'll be right over." She sounded brisk and managing. "We'd better get this straightened out. Whatever it is. Frankly, it sounds pretty wacky to me. If I hadn't met you up here— You didn't act like such a screwball, either today or that first time. What's got into you? Never mind. Tell me when I get there."

Ten minutes later she arrived. He ushered her in, feeling nervous and inadequate—as he often did with small, bossy women like Lulu, no matter what the circumstances. And of course these were special circumstances; not that Lulu showed any sign of thinking so. She marched into the living room, appraised it with one shrewd glance, sat down on the couch, and cocked her head at Martin with an air of good-humored inquiry.

"Now then, what's with you and Bob? Incidentally, you don't need to watch your language. Thelma's already told me all, as they say."

It didn't surprise him. In spite of Thelma's plea for silence on the subject of Bob, he had had a feeling she was going to tell Lulu herself. But in her own way, and without an audience. "And what did you make of it?" he asked.

"What is there to make of it? I gave her a good talking

to. That's what she expects from me. Poor Thelma, she's never grown up in some ways. Wants somebody to scold her for being naughty. I'm very fond of her, you know, and Vic's given her a pretty rough time. . . But that's neither here nor there. What I want to know is this business about Bob. My problem brother." She smiled wryly. "My no-good brother. Might as well admit it, I suppose. I don't give up easy, but he's too much for me. I checked him off a couple of years ago. Had to. It was either that or lose my happy home. Yes, and Mac was right. That's my husband, Mac. He gave Bob one last chance—against his better judgment, I talked him into it—and what does Bob do with it? Well, I won't go into details, but he was just damn lucky Mac didn't press charges or he'd have wound up in jail. I mean, what can you do with a character like that, even if he is your own brother?"

"Nothing. Check him off," said Martin. Only Lulu hadn't done that; she was too bossy and good-hearted to give up on anybody, ever. Scratch the Mrs. Richbitch veneer and you found a tough, misguided little missionary, incurably optimistic, and perfectly willing to lie—as she was doing now—if she had to.

"Right," said Lulu. "I don't know where you got the idea I could put you in touch with Bob. Surely not from Thelma. I shouldn't think from Vic, either." Her voice sharpened a little, on the name of Vic. No love lost between those two, Martin decided.

"As a matter of fact, it was from Bob's landlady. Former landlady, I should say. He cleared out last night. She said Bob talked a good deal about you, and that you were up there once, four or five months ago, to see him."

Lulu looked him straight in the eye and said, "Up

where? She's mistaken, this landlady. I didn't even know he was in New York till Thelma told me."

"I see. I was hoping you'd know where he moved to."

"Well, I don't. Why are you so anxious to get hold of him? Don't tell me, let me guess. He put the bite on you and skipped out without paying you back. Okay. How much?"

"No, no. It's not that. I didn't lend him any money."

"Congratulations." She tried, gamely, to smile. "So I guessed wrong. Money isn't the problem. I'm assuming there is a problem, from the look on your face. But maybe I'm wrong again, maybe that's your natural expression."

"There's a problem, all right. The reason I want to see Bob is to—well, in a way, to warn him. Otherwise he's apt to find himself in kind of a jam."

She blinked. Her eyes were round and clear, sherry-brown in color; one of her best points. "How bad a jam?" she asked.

"Bad. He's going to be accused of murdering Enid Baxter."

The shock of it made her gasp. But her back stayed straight, and her voice crisp. "That's absolutely ridiculous. You must be making it up. Nobody in their right mind would accuse Bob of—of— Why, he hardly knew Enid!"

"Maybe not, but he seems to have an abnormal interest in her death. He's brought this on himself, with all the snooping he's been doing. Somebody was bound to start suspecting that he knew Enid better than he's saying, or rather that he wanted to know her better than she wanted to know him."

"Oh my God," said Lulu. She closed her eyes and pressed her fingertips along the edge of her ash-blonde coiffure. For a moment only; and when she opened her eyes again they were bright with purpose. "Somebody. Who?"

"Who do you think?" He hoped she thought Martin, and to urge her along in this direction he folded his arms and assumed a stern expression. "Nothing's going to happen before tomorrow morning. After that—well, it depends on whether or not I can get hold of Bob and what he has to say for himself. If I don't find him the police will."

"You mean you'd actually go to the *police* with this crazy story? Why, they'll laugh in your face!"

"Remains to be seen," said Martin. "It seems to me they'll at least check up on what Bob was doing the night she was killed. I'm curious, myself. Because I can't believe he'd be all that interested unless he was mixed up in it, somehow or other. I'm not saying there isn't some other explanation. I'm just saying I want to hear it."

"This landlady you talked to. Didn't he leave a forwarding address with her?"

"He didn't even tell her he was moving. Simply picked up and left. That was to dodge Vic, I suppose."

"Not to mention bill collectors," Lulu said wearily. "Listen. He may be a bum, but he's not a murderer. And I'm not going to sit with folded hands and let you or anybody else call him one. No matter what. If I knew where to find him, I would. Do you believe me?"

"Yes," said Martin truthfully. His heart was thumping with excitement and triumph. The lever was working —on Lulu, never mind Bob—working better and more easily than he had dared to hope. He knew he was on the right track now.

"All right. Then here's something else for you to believe—"

The damn doorbell rang. They froze, staring at each other: Lulu lifting her brows in inquiry, Martin shaking his head and signalling silence. He was not going to answer, whoever it was.

Unless it was Bob? Once the possibility sprang up in his mind, he could not ignore it. He crept over to the window and peered out—straight into the face of Vic Holm, who had stopped ringing the doorbell and was now gripping the iron window bars in order to peer in.

Martin heaved a sigh—of regret, relief, which?—before he went to the door and opened it.

chapter 13

Vic breezed in, authoritative as ever, completely unabashed by the less than enthusiastic reception. "Hi, Lulu. Have a good cruise?" He gave her a perfunctory hug. "I found the note you left for Thelma. That's how I knew you were here. Forgive me for barging in on your little heart-to-heart with Martin, but something tells me it involves the Holms. Husband's intuition, I guess you'd call it."

Murderer's intuition was what Martin would call it. Vic was no fool: he must have sensed Martin's suspicions from the beginning, just as he must know now that time was running out. He could not risk any unsupervised heart-to-hearts; he had to know where he stood—not only with Martin, with everyone else too—in order to know what to do next. If he could not dodge disaster, he could at least meet it with his eyes open. It was odd, how much Martin knew about him in some ways. And how little, in others. For instance, did Vic even want to dodge disaster? It might be what he had craved all along, the destruction of himself, his true motive for destroying Enid. When the showdown came, would he welcome it? Or turn on Martin and fight for his life? He was a violent man, never mind the surface effect of calm security. And, unless Martin was way off course, he would soon be a desperate man, with nothing to lose.

He may kill me, Martin thought. He may very well kill me.

Meanwhile, here he sat in Martin's easy chair, legs stretched out, hands clasped behind his head, looking comfortable as a cat. "It's a funny thing, Lulu," he said sociably, "but Martin seems to get in on all the Holm family crises. I don't know whether Thelma's had time to fill you in on the latest installment or not—"

"She has," said Lulu. "And Martin's gone on from there. Congratulations on your intuition. You're involved in it, kid. Up to your neck, if you ask me."

"Sounds ominous." Vic smiled lazily. "You going to sue me for punching your poor little defenseless brother in the jaw? He had it coming. Now he knows what he's in for when he starts messing around with somebody else's wife."

"You're a fine one to talk. But don't get me started on that. It's not the point, anyway. A punch in the jaw—what's a little thing like that, compared with being accused of murder? Yes, you heard right. Murder. Martin thinks he killed Enid, don't ask me why or how, and. . ."

"Martin?" said Vic incredulously. He looked ready to burst out laughing; his eyes flicked toward Martin and away again, as if they shared a private joke.

Martin cleared his throat. "Now let's keep the record straight, Lulu. I didn't actually accuse Bob of murder.

But I do think he knows something about Enid's death, and I want to find out what. Time enough after I hear his story to decide whether or not I believe it and whether or not the police ought to hear it too."

"He might even tell you the truth," said Vic thoughtfully. "Scare him enough, and he probably will."

"That's what I'm counting on. The trouble is that so far I haven't been able to get hold of him. He moved last night, without leaving any forwarding address. Apparently one visit from you was enough."

"Yeah. I really fixed things, didn't I?" Again Martin caught the gleam of secret amusement in his eye. "Far be it from me to say a good word for a rat like Bob but honest to God, Martin, you're wasting your time trying to hang Enid's murder on him. I will admit, it's a lovely idea. Unfortunately, it won't work."

"Of course it won't," said Lulu. "I've been telling you the same thing. All right, I'm his sister, maybe I'm prejudiced, but Vic isn't. If he could help hang anything on Bob, don't worry, he'd do it. Nothing would please him more. You've got his word for it too. What more do you want?"

"Well, for one thing, I want to know how you can be so sure, both of you. If you haven't seen your brother in two years, how do you know what he's been up to? Same goes for Vic. He and Bob were barely acquainted, might not even have recognized each other if they'd met in the street. And that wasn't exactly a friendly call he paid on Bob last night. Yet he's firmly convinced Bob had nothing to do with Enid's death. So I want to know how Bob convinced him. It must have been a damn good story, and I want to hear it. One other thing, Lulu. I want to know what you were about to tell me when you were so rudely interrupted by the doorbell."

"You were about to tell Martin something?" Vic preserved his relaxed attitude. All the same, there was a difference, a sharpening of eye and tone. "Don't let me stop you. Or is it a secret?"

"Not from you," Lulu snapped back. "Are you going to tell him or am I? Because that's how it is. Sure I was going to tell him. You would too, if it was your brother."

"You flatter me. If it was my brother I'd have smothered him at birth. But not you. Not do-gooder Lulu. No cause too lost for you, is there?"

"Yes, there is. People like you." Lulu was on her feet, hopping mad, and sputtering like a feisty little dog tackling an enemy twice her size. "You're too selfish to live, Vic Holm. I always thought so, and now I know it. There's not one single solitary thing you care about except yourself. Never was and never will be. Selfish. Ungrateful. I may be a dimwit and a do-gooder, but you know as well as I do where Thelma would be if it hadn't been for me. Did you ever lift a finger to help her? Ha!"

"Okay, you've been a good friend to Thelma. I'm not denying it, and I appreciate it, incredible as it may seem to you. But don't forget, it worked both ways. You used Thelma as a cover-up, took advantage of her hospitality—and mine, without my knowing it—to sneak in your damn fool errands of mercy. And that I don't appreciate. You knew I wouldn't stand for it, that's why you did it behind my back. Don't talk to me about being selfish. Look at the mess you've got everybody into with your big-hearted lies."

"My lies! What about you, telling the police there was

nothing going on with you and Enid? You were lying your head off. I didn't think so then, and Thelma still doesn't, but—"

"But now you know." Vic waved his hand wearily. "Look, Lulu, you and I could go on sniping at each other forever and get no place. If you're going to tell Martin, tell him and get it over with."

"I'll be glad to." She whirled toward Martin, eyes flashing with tears, firm little front heaving. "All right. You want to know how I can be so sure about Bob. In the first place, it hasn't been two years since I saw him. As you've no doubt gathered. I meant to keep my word to my husband, but then Bob called me and I couldn't quite bring myself to cut him off. . . It was only money, and he swore he'd never ask me again. Of course he did. Thelma's known about it for quite a while, and after she moved here— It was her idea, she offered to. Bob would call her when he wanted to get in touch with me, and then she'd tell Vic we were going to the movies or something so I could nip off and meet him. She understood how I felt. It wasn't really hurting anybody, only I didn't dare let my husband know because he has this thing about Bob. Well." She drew a deep breath and burst out with it. "Well, the last time I saw him was the night Enid was killed. That's how I can be so sure."

"I see," said Martin. He looked at Vic, who was sitting forward in his chair now, staring at his feet. "And you didn't want your husband to find out, so you told the police you spent the whole evening in the Holms' apartment. In fact, all three of you lied to the police, because Vic and Thelma must have known you went out."

"Vic didn't," Lulu said quickly. "He went upstairs to bed right after dinner. We'd spent the afternoon at the beach, and the sun made him dopey. Besides, Thelma got started drinking, and when that happens he never sticks around if he can help it. Thelma did know. At least she knew I was planning to go out. We'd fixed it up between us to tell Vic our usual story, and then I'd leave her at the movies and slip off to see Bob. Only when the time came she was passed out. With Vic asleep upstairs, I figured it was safe, so I went anyway. It must have been about a quarter of ten when I left for 57th Street—Bob and I had arranged to meet at a bar up there—and I suppose it was about midnight when I got back. I remember Thelma was still laid out on the living room couch, but when I started undressing her she came to and reached for the bottle again. What a hassle! It's a wonder Vic didn't wake up."

"Not me," said Vic, with a one-sided grin. "I took a sleeping pill, just to make sure. I knew nothing about Lulu's excursion until Bob told me last night. As he'll tell you, if you still insist on tracking him down."

"But there's no point now, is there?" cried Lulu anxiously. "Bob's in the clear! No point in going to the police either. Surely you're satisfied now!"

Martin opened his mouth and shut it again. It was Vic who answered her, and he sounded not at all bitter—on the contrary, mild, even rather affectionate. "Lulu, Lulu, what about me and my alibi? It's blasted wide open."

"But nobody's accusing you of murder!"

"Nobody was. Maybe nobody will, but I doubt it. Our friend Martin isn't the type to shirk his civic duty. He's known all along that Enid and I were back together again. Now he knows I could have sneaked over here and killed her and sneaked back home with nobody the wiser. That's all he needs."

"I see," said Lulu. She sat down suddenly. "But I couldn't help it, Vic! I had to tell him!"

"Sure. Besides, he could be right. For all you know, he is."

"He can't be," she whispered. "If it had ever occurred to me, if I'd thought for one minute—I wouldn't have lied, no matter what."

"You didn't know then that I was back with Enid," Vic pointed out.

"All right, but I know now, and I still don't believe that you—that you—" She stared at him for a moment, then at Martin, then down at her sun-tanned, rosy-tipped hands. "Why should you?"

"Well, now, let me see. A lovers' quarrel, I expect. Right, Martin?"

Martin heard himself saying, explosively, "I want to talk to you. Alone." Nobody else's business. A private matter between him and Vic. They both looked at Lulu, who stood up as suddenly as she had sat down.

"Yes. All right." There was a miniature clashing of charm bracelet as she fumbled for her purse. But once at the door she stopped, undecided, perhaps frightened.

"Don't worry," said Vic. "I'm not dangerous."

"I was thinking about Thelma. It will all come out, won't it, about her and Bob?"

"Unless I can head Martin off, yes. And about you and Bob. That's your problem. Thelma and I will have to cope with our own. If you don't mind."

"I get it. 'Lulu Go Home.'" Her husky voice roughened. Almost broke. "Nothing else to do, I guess. If Mac's going to hear it anyway, better from me than otherwise. The worst part is Thelma. . ."

"She'll find your note when she gets home. I left it there. She'd probably call Martin anyway. I told you he gets in on all our family crises. So long, Lulu. Good luck."

"You too." This time her voice really did crack. Nothing left of it but a squeak. She shoved the door open and rushed out.

"Now," said Vic. He leaned back, once more assuming the classical attitude of relaxation: legs stretched out, hands clasped behind his head. "Before we get down to business, congratulations on the way you wangled the truth out of Lulu. Very neat. You could make a fortune on the state, boy. Damn near had me believing you suspected Bob. How did you happen to hit on that angle?"

"Rosemary. She does suspect him. That's how last night looked and sounded to her. I had to do some fast talking to keep her from going to the police right after lunch. So it wasn't really an act. One way or another, Lulu was going to be pressured into blasting your alibi. Yours and Thelma's, if you want to get technical."

"Not much point, is there? Thelma was in no shape to know what anybody else was doing, let alone do anything herself. We can rule her out and concentrate on me. I've had your vote from the start, haven't I? May I ask why?"

"Because Enid told me you might kill her. She foresaw what was going to happen, and it did."

The slanting light of late afternoon—that hazy, sad, religious light—struck the lower part of Vic's face, leaving his eyes cavernous and shadowy. The backward tilt of his head now seemed defenseless; Martin saw the chords in his neck tighten and felt a corresponding strain in his own throat. He went over to the bar and poured out two shots. When he turned around Vic was sitting forward, head bent, hands dangling between his knees.

"Thanks." He took the glass and stared at it absently. "But if she was afraid I might kill her. . ."

"I don't think she was afraid. She said if you ever did, it would be because she needled you into it." The words were Enid's own, and with them came an image of her in the brilliant-colored robe she had worn that night, preening herself like a bird, shamelessly playing Martin against Vic.

"She did?" Vic's eyes were fixed on his, searching, even now jealously intent on sharing whatever there was to be remembered about Enid. "When? How come she told you a thing like that?"

"The night I met you for the first time. Up at her place. You remember. You were going to the theater—" Vic nodded impatiently. "Well, that was when. We sat out on the terrace drinking brandy. She'd already told me a good deal about you. I don't know how come, maybe just because I was available. And lonesome, too. Anyway, we used to have these sessions. She'd talk about you, and I'd talk about Joyce."

"Who's Joyce?"

"My wife. She—died, a couple of years ago. Suddenly."

"Oh. I didn't know. Sorry. So you think Enid needled me into killing her."

"I think she refused to marry you. That was what you wanted. But she didn't, any more. It was different from Philadelphia. When you told me she'd agreed to marry you, you were just wishing. Well, not just wishing. You were also trying to cover up your motive."

"Got everything figured out, haven't you?" Vic discovered the drink in his hand; very thoughtfully, he took a sip. "All right. Let's say I had a motive. As far as you're concerned, that must clinch the case. Enid's premonition, motive, and now—thanks to Lulu—opportunity. What are you waiting for? If I had that much on you, believe me, I wouldn't be sitting here talking to you. I'd have gone to the cops long ago. Why the hell didn't you?"

Why indeed? It was going to sound ridiculous to Vic; the mixture of candid curiosity and contempt in his face made that clear. Martin felt himself flushing. "Because I promised Enid," he said curtly. "I'm sure a little thing like a promise wouldn't stop you, you'd have told the cops anyway. That's the difference between you and me."

"One of the differences. I'd never make such a promise in the first place. Unless you didn't take it seriously, this premonition of hers, or whatever you call it—"

"I took it seriously, all right. If I'd had my way she wouldn't ever have seen you again after that night. She knew herself it was a mistake."

"That's what you say. She went on seeing me, didn't she? In spite of wise old Father Martin's advice."

"Unfortunately, yes." Martin's slow burn suddenly broke into a blaze. "Damn it, can I help it if she elected me father confessor? I never wanted any part of any of this. You and Thelma and your domestic crises. I didn't ask her to land on my doorstep the other night and take her hair down. No, and I didn't ask to get in on that hassle you had with Bob. But I did get in on it, and now I'm stuck with it. I know too much. My God, how can I back out now?"

"It's your kind face. Your sympathetic nature. People can't resist opening their hearts to you."

"Can't resist lying to me, you mean. I'm not quite the idiot you and Thelma take me for."

"Thelma?" Vic switched off his comfortably derisive smile; he took another sip of his drink.

"Of course Thelma. Just give me enough time, and eventually I get the pitch, even with an expert like Thelma. No, expert's not the right word. She's been lying out of desperation, frantically trying to cover up for you. Because she must have guessed it was you from the beginning and God help her she loves you. So she lied about herself and Bob. Actually, I fed her her lines. All she had to do was feed them back to me."

Vic waited, watching him steadily.

"The affair with Bob was a myth. It's perfectly obvious now what was going on between them. He wasn't romancing her, he was blackmailing her. In a modest way. He didn't dare push too hard, because it was to his own interest, as well as everybody else's, to keep his mouth shut about the night Enid was killed. He didn't want Lulu's husband finding out she was still giving him handouts; it would mean the end of the handouts, and in the long run Lulu was his best bet. On the other hand, he couldn't quite pass up the chance to put the bite on Thelma for a little extra, especially with the life line to Lulu temporarily disconnected while she was off on her cruise."

"Pretty shaky grounds for blackmail, if you ask me."

"Very shaky. He knew better than to try it on you. But it worked with Thelma. She was too scared to tell you —she couldn't bring herself to admit she suspected you of murder. And too scared to call Bob's bluff—she couldn't be sure it was a bluff, he might talk, out of spite if nothing else. She did what he counted on her doing. She panicked and paid."

"To cover up for me," Vic murmured. "Because God

help her she loves me. You're right, you know. She does. God help us both." He got up and prowled aimlessly about the room. Finally he stopped in front of Martin. But what he said was, after all, a triviality. "You didn't tell Lulu. About the blackmailing business. Evidently Thelma didn't either."

"Nor you."

"No. She's not a bad little Indian, you know. In spite of everything."

"She should have been a missionary," said Martin, and there they were, smiling at each other in one of their flashes of comradeship. Once more he felt the inner swing, like a pendulum, between like and dislike, trust and mistrust, rapport and antagonism.

"I'm going to keep my promise to Enid," he said. "Whatever else I tell, it won't be that."

"I know it. What do you want, a vote of thanks?"

"No, I want you to understand. I want to explain. . ." The face above him, the deceptively open face, the strange, hazy eyes—friend or enemy, what was the difference? The bond between them remained. "It's because of Joyce."

"Joyce? Oh yes, your wife. How do you mean, because of her?"

"They said I killed her. Her family. They don't think it was an accident. They said I pushed her."

"I see," said Vic gravely. "So that's why. You know how it feels."

"I know how it feels. I know you can love somebody and still want to kill them."

Vic licked his lips. "Well. And did you? Kill her, I mean?"

"I don't know," said Martin, as he had said—how long

ago?—to Enid; as he had almost said to Rosemary. "They said I pushed her, and I could have. I'm not sure I didn't. I simply don't know."

("That's impossible," Enid had told him irritably. "Of course you know. Of course you didn't kill her. You've worked yourself into a guilt complex brooding about it. It's exactly like you." Rosemary would have said much the same thing. You and your soul searching, Rosemary would have said.)

But Vic understood that it was possible. That was part of the bond between them: they both knew all about guilt. He nodded. His hand even reached out in what might have been a gesture of compassion. An uncompleted gesture. The next instant the pendulum took another swing, and he was turning away, once more arrogant and mocking.

"For a guy who doesn't know what he did himself, you're awfully damn sure about me. You get the benefit of the doubt but I don't. Is that right?"

"Right. I've stretched all the points I'm going to. I intend to keep my word to Enid, but that doesn't mean her murderer gets away with it."

"I could keep you from going to the cops, you know." Casually, Vic took a gun out of his pocket and put it on the end table beside him. There it lay, blunt-nosed and loaded with death, between the ash tray and Martin's breakfast coffee cup.

Martin swallowed hard. "You won't get away with killing me, either. Too many other people know too much. Lulu, for one."

"I might figure it was worth it anyway. Did you ever think of that?"

"I'd rather not," Martin said, and—incredibly—a grin

flickered between them. "There's the doorbell. Do I answer it or not?"

"It's Thelma." Vic's face suddenly looked haggard. Between urgent peals of the bell her voice reached them, excitedly calling Martin's name.

"Go ahead," said Vic. "Let her in."

chapter 14

"Vic!" She whipped past Martin and skidded to a stop in the middle of the room. Her bangs were plastered to her forehead with sweat; the rest of her hair, never very firmly anchored, straggled about her face. She was out of breath—she must have run all the way—and her eyes looked like a frightened horse's. "Lulu told me," she panted. "She was there when I got home, she came back for her bag, and she told me— It's not true? Martin? You're not going to—"

"It's true." Vic got up and led her over to the couch. Then he went back to his own post. Beside the gun. Had she seen it? No. She had eyes for nothing but Vic. "You did your best for me, Thelma, but it's no use lying any more. Martin's got everything figured out."

She doubled over, as if in physical pain, pressing her head against her knees; Martin saw the ridges of her knuckles as she gripped the edge of the couch. When she straightened up, the miracle had been achieved: she was in control of herself. "I'd like a cigarette," she said, and Martin sprang to light one for her. "Thanks. Sit down and listen to me, Martin. I can't let you do this. It's terrible. A terrible mistake. First of all, there's a difference between lying and just not mentioning something. Isn't there? Well. That's all Lulu and I did when they asked us, you know, about that night. We just didn't mention that she went out to meet Bob. Not on Vic's account, believe me, but on Lulu's. It never even crossed our minds that—"

"I said it's no use." Vic seemed to be speaking between clenched teeth. "He knows you weren't having an affair with Bob. It was blackmail. Lulu doesn't know it, but he does. I told you, he's got everything figured out."

Her eyes closed briefly, then opened wide. They looked deep and dark as the ocean. "All right. Yes. I did lie about that." Her face trembled into a smile. "You gave me the idea, Martin. Just as you gave Bob the blackmailing idea. You and Rosemary. When he went back to The Peacock to get his sketch pad and you were still there. That's when it started, that's when he got off on the Enid project."

"But you were there with him earlier. He must have already made his pitch for money."

"For a loan, a nice, innocent little loan to tide him over while Lulu was away. That's all it was when he called me the first time and I agreed to meet him. I couldn't let him come to the apartment, you see, because Vic didn't know about his arrangement with Lulu. Then we ran smack into you and Rosemary and I had to say something, so I made up the murals, Bob White instead of Black, don't tell Vic, it's a surprise." She pulled dreamily on her cigarette. "But it was a different story, after he went back to get his sketch pad. He had something else in mind. Oh no, it wasn't just an innocent little loan any more."

No, it wouldn't be, thought Martin. He remembered the careful way Bob had set down his glass when Enid's name was mentioned; his own obscure alarm at having mentioned it; Rosemary's sigh: "I wish I hadn't talked so much." What a package of goodies they had handed Bob! How his heart must have leapt when he heard about everybody's alibis and realized what he could do to two of them! He had not made the connection before; why should he? The newspaper accounts of Enid's death named no names. Lulu, the Holms, Martin—all had been lumped together as "the dead woman's friends," who had produced no leads when questioned by the police.

"He didn't come out with it right away," Thelma was going on. "Not until after he'd tried pumping everybody he could think of. All he did that first night was drop a few hints. About Vic and Enid. It was enough for me. I knew what he was working up to and I couldn't face it. All I could think of to do was have another drink, get lost, disappear, not be there next time he called. It didn't work, of course. You always have to come back and face everything. I took the long way round, I stopped here first. Crazy, isn't it, but I had this notion that I might even be able to tell you the truth. Only—"

"Only I gave you the idea for another lie, so you told me that instead."

"And you sent me home with Vic. And Bob called the next day and I pawned my jewelry and paid him. Yesterday? It seems so much longer ago." She looked down at her outstretched hands. Her diamond, and her wedding band, which had been missing at lunch, were now back in place. "I redeemed them this afternoon. That's where I went after Lulu came. After lunch. It was fun, wasn't it? We had a good time, didn't we?"

"You had a good time lying," said Martin. Too good a time. She would have done better to omit the innuendos against Bob. For they had precipitated this crisis. Without them to trigger Rosemary into action—threatened action—and through her Martin, he might still be dragging his feet and searching his soul. But surely not for much longer? No, of course not. The pressure of all he knew and suspected would have forced him (even him, a reluctant hunter if there ever was one) into cornering his quarry, one way or another. No escape, for either Vic or him.

Or for Thelma. What could she do but go on lying? That had been the point of the luncheon party—to find out what Martin and Rosemary made of the night before and tailor her lies to fit. It must have given her a nasty shock to learn that they knew who Bob really was. But she had carried on. Was carrying on now. Would continue to carry on, as long as she had the breath left to lie with.

"Lying, yes. But in a good cause," she said, and sent a glowing look across the room to Vic.

He received it impassively.

Martin felt his temper rising. "A good cause. For God's sake, Thelma! You must have suspected Vic yourself or you wouldn't have paid Bob off."

"Why must I? Why couldn't I have been looking out for little old me? Vic wasn't the only one that would be left without an alibi if Bob talked. And when it comes to motive, I had more reason for wanting her dead than Vic had. He loved her. I—hated her." She lingered over the word, cherishing it. "I knew, of course. Vic didn't have to tell me. When I saw her at that press party, I knew how it was going to be. And it was. Oh yes, if anybody had a motive it was me."

"It's not quite that simple," Martin began, "because Enid wasn't—"

But Vic cut in unceremoniously. "This is all beside the point. Nobody's going to take you seriously, Thelma, motive or no motive. You were falling down drunk that night. In no shape to do anything yourself or know what I did. How many times do I have to tell you it's no use trying to convince Martin? He won't believe a word you say. Neither will I."

"No?" She smiled off into space. "You don't believe I hated her? Your beautiful little brainy little bitch?"

"So you hated her. I said motive or no motive."

"Yes. Falling down drunk, you said. That isn't like you, Vic. You always used to call it my drinking problem. My dear departed drinking problem. I was in unusually good form that night, wasn't I? It was an inspired performance."

There was a brief, twanging silence. Then Martin said, "So that's your pitch, is it? You weren't really drunk. Just putting on an act."

"You think I couldn't have?" She sprang up, smiling mischievously. For a moment only: all at once her face sagged into drunken vacuity, her eyes went bleary, her legs rubbery. She lurched and mumbled and finally melted back onto the couch, head lolling, toes up, wrists boneless. No doubt about it, she looked plastered. "Just a sample. I can do even better when I put my mind to it. Sometimes, of course, it was for real. It always was, at first. But then I discovered how easy it was to fake it, and how convenient. . . You see what a terrible mistake you're making, Martin? It doesn't have to be Vic. It could just as easily have been me."

"Maybe the police will buy that. I won't," said Martin stubbornly.

"Neither will I," Vic said, but after a noticeable pause. And he was watching her with peculiar intensity. Suddenly, violently, he smacked his hands down on the arms of his chair. "Stop trying to help me! Do me a favor and stop this crazy lying! Martin thinks I killed her and that's the end of it. He knows more than he's told you—"

"What? What hasn't he told me? I have a right to know."

"For one thing, he knows you can want to kill somebody you love. For another, he knows—he's figured out a whiz of a motive, especially for me. And just to make everything perfect, he knows that Enid halfway expected me to kill her. She had no secrets from wise old Father Martin. He had none from her. And they always kept their promises to each other."

"She told him you were going to kill her?" Thelma gave an ugly laugh. "Yes. Typical. Exactly like her, to frame you in advance."

"That's not true." Martin and Vic said it in unison, once more trapped into uneasy collaboration. Vic went on, in a withering-cold voice. "Nobody's interested in your views on Enid. You don't know a damn thing about her or how she felt about me."

"Oh, don't I!" The color blazed up in Thelma's face. "It's beyond my ken, is it, this immortal love of yours and Enid's, too sacred for the likes of me. She wasn't going to marry you! That's how much she loved you. She wouldn't have you as a gift! If you want to know how. . ." She gulped into silence, like a child frightened by the force of her own tantrum. Her brief, costly triumph was turning visibly into terror. Vic had risen deliberately, and now towered over her; she shrank back against the couch cushions as if she expected him to hit her.

"Yes," he said softly, "I'm very much interested in how you happen to know that. I never told you."

But he must have. Must have confessed everything to her, knowing that he could count on her loyalty, even in the face of murder. No wonder she was terrified at having lost her temper and blurted out the confirmation of what Martin knew anyway, the "whiz of a motive" he had figured out for Vic.

"Martin told you, didn't he?" Vic demanded, still softly. "It's his theory. Of course. That's how you know. Thelma?"

She had never looked more vulnerable, more openly at the mercy of her feelings than in that long moment of hesitation while she stared up at Vic, loving him, fearing him as much as she feared for him. Then her eyes shifted to Martin, and the scales were tipped. She shook her head. "Enid told me," she whispered. "Now will you believe it was me, not Vic?"

Without a word Vic turned on his heel and went back to his chair. He sat down heavily. He waited, poker faced.

"I don't—I—" Stop stuttering, Martin told himself. You knew it was coming. Knew she was going to pull a phoney confession act if she couldn't find any other way to clear Vic. It is a phoney. She's lying her head off. As usual. And Vic's letting her. The bastard. "You tell me, Vic," he said. "Should I believe her?"

"No!" Vic himself seemed startled by the one vehement

word he had loosed. His voice sank to a murmur. "No. Of course not. Impossible."

"Why is it impossible?" cried Thelma. "You were sound asleep upstairs. Lulu left without your hearing her. How do you know I didn't go out too?"

"Are you saying you did? Because if I thought you killed her, Thelma, so help me, I'd—"

"Kill me?" she began to laugh hysterically. "Yes, kill me, I'd wind up like her, murdered, it's been happening all my life, I take on other people's afflictions. . . It's such a funny word to use for being murdered, isn't it? Affliction? Like calling war the recent unpleasantness. . ."

"Sh," said Martin. He gave her a little shake, and she subsided. "Okay, maybe it's not a physical impossibility. You could have faked the drunk act and gone to see Enid that night. You've got no more of an alibi than Vic has. But you've got no motive, either. If what you claim is true—that she told you she wouldn't have Vic as a gift—then why on earth should you kill her? You had nothing to fear from her. She wasn't going to break up your marriage. So why—"

"No, she did that four years ago," said Thelma bitterly. "I wouldn't admit it at the time, but she did, she reduced it to rubble, and even that wasn't enough for her. This time it was going to be Vic himself. I couldn't stand it, I couldn't—I'd do anything for him, I'd even give him up, and all she did was sneer. Don't you see? It wasn't just sneering at me, it was Vic too, it was everything I've lived for." She paused, and finished in a different, hushed tone, "So cruel. Oh, she had such a mean tongue."

And that at least was true. Martin could imagine the scene—fictitious though it surely was; look at the glaze of self-hypnosis in Thelma's eyes—in all its galling detail. Enid would have shown no mercy; she had a sure instinct for the word that would cut deepest. A way, as Vic had said, of belting you with things just when you were in no shape to take them. And Enid herself: I never do the right thing except at the wrong moment.

All right. But it took some doing to go on and imagine Thelma snatching up the knife and ramming it home. Violence was Vic's native land; Thelma lived in a world of devious side steppings and labyrinthine lies. This last tale was only more of the same. No matter how adroitly she twisted the facts, Vic's motive remained stronger than hers. She had said it herself only a moment ago: she would do anything for him. Even to giving him up. Even to confessing to his crime. And there he sat, not only letting her do it, but threatening to kill her if she made it convincing enough.

It was probably an idle threat, intended as clinching proof of Vic's innocence. One more stroke in the image he was trying to project of himself as Enid's avenger instead of her murderer. And yet. . .

As if he sensed the trend of Martin's thoughts, Vic switched on the table lamp beside him, dispelling the shadows of dusk. The gun sprang into view; Thelma saw it and stiffened.

"I'm prepared, you see," he said. "I have been, ever since Enid was murdered. I don't care what she was or what she was going to do to me. I just want to get my hands on whoever killed her." He caught Martin's eye on him, and smiled his sudden, warm smile. "No exceptions. Not even myself. But then I've never suspected myself. I leave that to you, Martin."

Martin sat silent and unsmiling, reminding himself that

he had invited this sort of double-edged crack (and a pretty good one, too) when he chose to confide his own secret guilt to Vic. Chose? He had no choice; circumstances, and the fitful, ghostly comradeship between him and Vic had combined to draw it out of him. The ultimate in foolish futility: he had experienced no healthful catharsis, and Vic had certainly not responded with an outpouring of his own. But then Martin had not expected anything like that. Vic was too cagey. And too arrogant even to bother denying his guilt. This was as close as he had come to it.

"I'm not afraid, Vic," said Thelma with calm assurance. "You won't kill me. Because—"

"Because he knows you didn't do it," Martin broke in. "Nobody better. No. That would be carrying the bluff a bit too far. Even for him."

Neither of them took any notice; once more Vic was watching her with that strange fixity. It did not unnerve her. She met it with a steady, challenging stare of her own. "Because I'm the one you really love. Me. Not her. If I hadn't known that, I would have let you go, four years ago. Because I'm the one that really loves you too. She didn't. You were just the Great Might-Have-Been to her. That's all. She couldn't forgive you for staying with me. She was going to get even with you if it killed her. And it did, it did. Martin's right, you know. If I hadn't killed her you would have."

"No!" Again Vic loosed the single violent word. It throbbed and died away. He went on hoarsely, "You're lying. That's where Martin's right. You're lying to get me off the hook. It's all a lot of—"

"You want me to prove it? All right then, I will." She sprang up, so white-faced and trembling, with such a wild blaze in her eyes, that Martin and Vic jumped to their feet in alarm. "You think I didn't hate her enough? You don't know, oh, you don't know. . . I'll show you. Look. Come on. Both of you." She darted across to the window sill where three of Enid's potted plants still sat, waiting to be transplanted. Snatching up the begonia, she turned and thrust it at Vic. "Here. See for yourself."

"See for myself? It's just a plant of some kind, a what-do-you-call-it—"

"Oh, is it! Is it! You don't believe it's special, the only one of its kind. It doesn't show till you pull it up. You think I'm crazy, don't you? So humor me. Pull it up."

"Oh, what the hell," said Vic, and wrenched the plant free of its pot. Dirt crumbled to the floor from the packed roots. Impatiently he gave it a little shake, and there was a different sound, a muted, metallic rattle.

They stared down at Enid's jade ring, missing no longer. After a moment Martin stooped and picked it up. He looked from Vic's drawn, blank face to Thelma's, which was set in a smile of terrible triumph. Above the roaring in his ears he heard her saying, "Now will you believe I killed her? You gave it to her. That's why I took it. I hid it here the night you came and got me, after Bob. . . I thought it was all up with me then. It never occurred to me anybody would suspect you. Or that you wouldn't. . . Vic!" Her voice rose sharply; she began stumbling backward in jerky, clumsy steps. "It was for you, Vic! I did it for you!"

Too late, Martin saw Vic's face, the ponderous lowering of his head, like a bull getting ready to charge. Too late, he made a grab for the gun; Vic's arm shot out and spun him halfway across the room to crash against the couch. When he picked himself up the gun was in Vic's hand and he was moving deliberately toward Thelma, who stood frozen in piteous, incredulous panic.

"Don't!" yelled Martin, and hurled the footstool. It smacked against Vic's shoulder. Harmlessly, but in the moment that he was off balance Thelma whirled and scrambled out into the hall. Instantly noise erupted: a dog's shrill barking, and a thready old voice vainly demanding quiet. Through the open door Martin saw the familiar figures of Bubbles and Mrs. Klein—the one rotund and fuzzy, the other frail and rain-coated—just coming in the street door, blocking Thelma's way out.

That left the stairs; she fled up them at breakneck speed, as she must have fled down them that night—very fast, Mrs. Klein had reported, very hard—accompanied then as now by Bubbles' frantic racket.

It was hopeless, of course. Vic was already after her. Martin felt himself shoved aside and heard the thick, labored breathing and then the other, heavier footsteps. He watched from the foot of the stairs, rooted there in nightmare fascination. For he seemed to be not only spectator but actor. His own chest ached with the fury of pursuit; the stairs he was looking at dissolved into the rough, moonlit path to the quarry, along which he pounded, oblivious to everything but Joyce up ahead, in her disaster-green dress. . . Did it matter that there had been no gun in his hand? He could still have had murder in his heart.

"No," he whispered, and the path, the quarry, vanished; it was two other people on a stairway.

At the landing Thelma stopped running and turned to face Vic and the gun. In despair? She knew the stairway was a blind alley and she would be trapped at the top if not before. Or was it in hope? She might still believe that he loved her too much to kill her. Love her he must; or he would not have struggled so long and obstinately against the fact of her guilt. For unlike Martin, he knew that he himself was innocent. Yet he too had insisted she was lying. For his sake. Everything had been for him. If he could still kill her, knowing that, then. . .

Then the basis of her whole life was delusion, and Enid was the winner, after all.

For whatever reason, she stopped running and turned. Vic stopped too, arrested in mid-step; with one hand grasping the banister and his head tilted back, he seemed, illogically, the more defenseless of the two. On the landing Thelma waited, poised in unearthly tranquility. In the instant he fired, she lifted her arms, as if to embrace him and death, the two together. Then she toppled and slumped down in a graceless heap.

Behind Martin, Bubbles abandoned himself to complete hysteria, while Mrs. Klein offered a quavering obligato: "Mr. Shipley, Mr. Shipley. . ."

He started up the stairs; Vic was already at the landing. "Don't come up here." He still had the gun; he gestured with it imperiously. "Stay away from me."

Martin stayed where he was.

"She's dead. I killed her. Martin, I—"

"I know," said Martin.

"Yes. All right. Then don't try to stop me." There he crouched, a murderer at last, but peremptory as always, a little contemptuous of Martin, and a little admiring. Behind the desolation in his eyes Martin caught the old flicker; once more they were drawn together in unlikely, unwilling rapport. "Don't try to stop me," Vic repeated.

"I won't," said Martin. He would have promised, even

without the gun. There ought to be something more to say. But there wasn't. He went back down the stairs.

The second shot came before he reached the door of his own apartment. He stopped, shivering, but not with surprise. He had known Vic was going to do it.

It was what he would have done, too, if he had killed Joyce.